Nw
Rom
M MJ

ROMANCE

Large Print Che
Chesney, Marion.
The romance

WITHDRAWN

JUN 10 1998

THE ROMANCE

Marion Chesney

Being the Fifth Volume of
The Daughters of Mannerling

Chivers Press ● G.K. Hall & Co.
Bath, England   Thorndike, Maine USA

This Large Print edition is published by Chivers Press, England, and by G.K. Hall & Co., USA.

Published in 1998 in the U.K. by arrangement with Lowenstein Associates Ltd.

Published in 1998 in the U.S. by arrangement with St. Martin's Press.

U.K. Hardcover ISBN 0–7540–3197-7 (Chivers Large Print)
U.S. Softcover   ISBN 0–7838–8385-4 (Nightingale Series Edition)

The text of this Large Print edition is unabridged.
Other aspects of the book may vary from the original edition.

Set in 16 pt. New Times Roman.

Printed in Great Britain on acid-free paper.

British Library Cataloguing in Publication Data available

Library of Congress Cataloging-in-Publication Data

Chesney, Marion.
    The romance / Marion Chesney.
    p. (large print) cm. — (The daughters of Mannerling ; 5th v.)
    ISBN 0-7838-8385-4 (sc. : alk. paper)
    1. Large type books.   2. Inheritance and succession—England—
Fiction. 3. Young women—England—Fiction.   4. England—
Social life and customs—19th century—Fiction.   I. Title.
II. Series: Chesney, Marion. Daughters of Mannerling ; 5th v.
    [PR6053.H4535R66   1998]
    823' . 914-dc21   97-32594

*This series is dedicated to Rosemary Barradell,
with love.*

CHAPTER ONE

Taking numbers into account, I think more mental suffering had been undergone in the streets leading from St. George's, Hanover Square, than in the condemned cells of Newgate.
　　　　　　　　　　　　—*SAMUEL BUTLER*

The two remaining Beverley sisters, Belinda and Lizzie, were in London for the Season, far from their country home, and far from their family obsession with Mannerling, the house they loved, the house they had been evicted from due to their late father's gambling debts.

Their four elder sisters had all married well. Belinda and Lizzie were staying with Abigail, Lady Burfield, one of their sisters, at her town house.

One cold spring morning, they were walking with their maid, Betty, through Hanover Square, when Lizzie cried, 'There is a wedding at Saint George's. Let's go and look.'

'Such a press of people,' grumbled Belinda.

'Oh, let's see if the bride looks as pretty as you are going to look when you marry Lord Saint Clair.' Lord St. Clair, reported to be resident in London, and the new owner of Mannerling, was the target of Belinda's ambitions, although she had not yet met him. Marriage to the owner of Mannerling would mean getting their old home back.

They edged their way gingerly through the throng of sight seers, gingerbread men, and orange sellers. The church bells were clanging out across sooty London.

'Here comes the bride,' said Belinda, and then gave a little gasp.

A young girl came out on the arm of a portly old man.

'Is that her father?' asked Lizzie, puzzled. 'He's supposed to lead her in, not out.'

'It's her husband,' said Belinda gloomily.

The groom was heavy-set with a bloated face. His silk wedding clothes were strained across his figure. His bride might have appeared prettier were not her face blotched with crying. She was trembling and her large eyes roamed this way and that as if seeking escape. The crowd fell silent.

Still silent, they watched as the girl was led to the gaily decorated bridal carriage. A footman helped her in, and she sat with her head bent. Her groom heaved himself in beside her. He tossed money to the crowd, who surged forward and scrabbled for pennies.

'Come away,' said Belinda. They edged their way slowly through the press. The bells continued to ring out triumphantly. Lizzie shivered. She thought their brazen mouths were calling out in celebration of greed and folly and vanity rather than ringing down God's blessing on a marriage.

'It happens, Lizzie,' said Belinda gently, 'marriages are always being arranged for money.'

'We in society are supposed to be so sensitive, so cultured, so refined,' said Lizzie, 'and yet ladies are forced to behave no better than the trulls at Covent Garden who solicit the gentleman for little more than a shilling and a glass of gin.'

'It is no one we know, Lizzie.'

'Are we any better?' demanded Lizzie fiercely. 'We do not know this Lord Saint Clair. What if he is a gambler, an oaf, and a wastrel? Would you marry him then just to regain Mannerling?'

'No, of course not, silly,' said Belinda. But he is reported to be only in his early twenties and we have heard no scandal about him.'

'But should he be offensive in any way,' urged Lizzie, 'you will not go ahead with this marriage?'

Belinda giggled. 'I have not even met the gentleman yet, stoopid. He may take one look at me and walk away.'

'No one could walk away from your beauty,' said Lizzie simply.

And Belinda did turn heads in the street. She had jet-black hair and creamy skin, large eyes, and a dainty figure. All the Beverley sisters, except waiflike little Lizzie with her red hair, were accounted beauties. Lizzie reflected that as each sister had contemplated marriage, she had grown in beauty. Lizzie hoped that the same miracle would happen to her when her time came.

Sometimes she hated Mannerling for the almost supernatural grip the stately house had on her. And yet a stubborn illogical voice in her head would tell her that if only they could get their old home back again, with its cool rooms, its painted ceilings, and long green lawns, then life would be peaceful and content.

From the drawing-room window of Abigail's town house, the girls' governess, Miss Trumble, watched them return from their walk. She gave a little sigh. Two still to go. Two more Beverley daughters to find suitable husbands for. She wondered if they still were obsessed with Mannerling.

Lady Beverley came into the drawing-room with one long, white, ringed hand to her forehead. 'I am feeling unwell, Miss Trumble. You will need to chaperone Belinda and Lizzie to the Tamworths' musicale tonight.'

'What about Lady Burfield?'

'It is not Abigail's job to take care of Lizzie and Belinda. Besides, my son-in-law and daughter have another engagement. I do not know why you are so reluctant to go out into society, Miss Trumble.'

Miss Trumble smiled but did not reply. Lady Beverley looked at the elderly governess with some irritation. Miss Trumble had a stately air about her, her brown hair had not a trace of

4

grey in it and was dressed expertly in one of the new Roman styles, and her gown was of fine silk. What Lady Beverley disliked most about her was that Miss Trumble sometimes made *her* feel like the servant.

'I am ordering you to escort them,' she said coldly, 'and that is that.'

After she had left the room, Belinda and Lizzie came in. 'How was your walk?' asked Miss Trumble.

'Rather sad,' said Lizzie, taking off her bonnet and swinging it by its ribbons. 'We saw a wedding at Saint George's. Such a young lady being wed to a horrible old man.'

'Just be grateful that you never have to suffer the same fate. I am to escort you this evening.'

'Mama is unwell again?' asked Belinda.

'I think your mother has a headache,' said Miss Trumble, keeping her opinion to herself that there was nothing up with Lady Beverley at all. Mrs. Tamworth, who was giving the musicale that evening, had remarked to Lady Beverley at a ball the previous week that it was sad to see the Beverley family fallen on such hard times. This comment had taken all Lady Beverley's pride in having four daughters successfully wed away from her, and she had promptly taken Mrs. Tamworth in dislike.

'Are you enjoying London?' Miss Trumble asked.

Belinda sighed. 'It is all very exciting and yet I often wish I were back at home. Being brought out is an onerous business. What if no gentleman proposes marriage?'

'Then you try again the following year,' remarked Miss Trumble.

Lizzie's green eyes gleamed with amusement. 'And if Belinda does not take then, will she be sent to India to catch the eye of some jaded officer at the Calcutta Season? That is the way of the world.'

'Belinda has already caught the eye of about every gentleman in London,' said Miss Trumble. 'I can only hope she will find someone to fall in love with, as her elder sisters have done.'

'Love?' Belinda fidgeted fretfully with the fringe of her shawl. 'What is love?'

'It is an emotion powerful enough to banish hopes of Mannerling from silly minds,' said Miss Trumble sharply.

She noticed with a sinking heart the way the girls exchanged glances. Miss Trumble hoped this Lord Saint Clair, the new owner of Mannerling, would not be present at the musicale, or indeed at any other function that the girls attended.

*   *   *

Later that day, Miss Trumble walked up to the attics, where Barry Wort, the Beverleys' odd man from the country, had a room. She scratched at the door and heard his voice call,

'Come in.'

Barry looked up, a smile creasing his features as the governess walked into the room.

Miss Trumble smiled back, thinking again what a rock Barry was in a shifting world. He was an ex-soldier who tended the garden and did all the rough work at the Beverleys' home, Brookfield House. He was a sturdy figure with grey hair and a round, pleasant, honest face.

Miss Trumble sat down. 'We have not had much time for conversation, Barry.'

'No, miss. I was thinking of asking my lady if I might return to the country. There is no work for me here. I have seen all the sights and now I am anxious to return.'

'I wish I could go with you,' said Miss Trumble. 'I am to escort Belinda and Lizzie to a musicale this evening. My lady is indisposed, although the real fact is that she has taken this evening's hostess in dislike.'

Barry looked at her shrewdly. 'You have hitherto been loath to appear in society.'

'Nonsense. Only your imagination. It is not my place to chaperone the girls. Goodness knows what Mrs. Tamworth will say when she sees I am come instead of Lady Beverley. Have you any news of this Lord Saint Clair, the new owner of Mannerling?'

'Only a little bit here and here. A Bond Street beau, foppish, but nothing very scandalous.'

'I only hope Belinda has not the foolish idea

7

of trying to wed him, but there is something secretive these days about Lizzie and Belinda. That cursed house, that wretched Mannerling. Will it never let them go?'

'It's only a house, I reckon,' said Barry soothingly. 'It's them that won't let it go. They do say, though, that the place is haunted by Judd and Cater.' Judd, a previous owner, had hanged himself from the chandelier in the great hall. Cater, a sugar-plantation owner, who had proposed to Rachel Beverley and been refused, had disappeared. Unknown to Miss Trumble, Barry, and the Beverleys, he had been drowned.

'Let us just pray that Belinda meets someone suitable,' said Miss Trumble. 'I shall miss you, Barry.'

'I'll return soon, miss, but I would feel more comfortable back at my usual work.'

Miss Trumble rose to her feet. Barry looked at her curiously. 'What will you do after they are all wed? Stay as companion to Lady Beverley?'

'I think not.'

'Then what?'

She smiled. 'I will think of something.'

*   *   *

Belinda and Lizzie stared in amazement at their governess that evening when they met her in the drawing-room preparatory to setting out for the musicale. For Miss Trumble looked very odd indeed and not at all like her elegant self. Not only was she sporting a large black wig but her face looked puffed up and distorted.

'Why are you wearing a wig?' cried Lizzie. 'And surely you are wearing wax pads in your cheeks. No one does that any more.' There had been a fashion, recently exploded, for ladies to wear wax pads in their cheeks to give their faces a Dutch-doll effect.

'It is almost as if you don't want to be recognized,' complained Belinda.

'I will do very well,' said Miss Trumble. 'No one looks at an old chaperone.'

Belinda and Lizzie were both wearing white muslin gowns, Belinda's being the more elaborate of the two, having more flounces at the hem and a wide embroidered satin sash at the waist. She was wearing one of the new Turkish turbans on her black hair, bought for her at great expense by her sister Abigail. Lizzie wore a wreath of silk leaves and artificial roses.

'Come,' said Miss Trumble. 'It will be a quiet evening, and with any luck the music will be pleasant.'

*　　　*　　　*

Mrs. Tamworth, a grand figure with rouged cheeks and Prince of Wales feathers in her pomaded hair, was not pleased that Lady

Beverley had sent this peculiar elderly creature with the odd wig in her place. She nodded haughtily to Miss Trumble and said in a loud, carrying voice, 'Do tell Lady Beverley I consider her behaviour strange.'

She looked over Miss Trumble's shoulder. 'Ah, Lord Saint Clair is arrived.'

Lizzie would have turned around, but Belinda pinched her arm and whispered, 'Do not look in the least bit interested, or Miss Trumble will lecture us.'

They took their seats among the chattering company. Many of the gentlemen promptly stood up again to get a better look at Belinda, but Belinda was unaware of their interest. Her heart was beating hard. If only she knew what Lord St. Clair looked like. When the company had settled again and the musicale was about to begin, Belinda raised her fan to her face and took a covert look around.

And then she was sure she saw him, a tall, handsome man with hair as black as her own, a strong face and proud nose and sherry-coloured eyes. She had heard that Lord St. Clair was a fashionable beau, and this man was dressed in the finest tailoring. He made every other man in the room look either overdressed or shoddy. Why, just look at that peacock of a young man next to him with his corseted waist, his fobs and seals, his cravat so starched and so high he could barely turn his head.

The first performer was an opera singer, a

10

large woman with a clear sweet voice. Belinda gave herself up to the beauty of the music and for the time being forgot about Mannerling and Lord St. Clair.

The opera singer was followed by a pianist who played Mozart with verve. Belinda glanced along the room to where the handsome man sat. He was perfectly still, wrapped in the music. Beside him the fop—what a contrast!—fidgeted and yawned.

A rosy dream began to take hold of Belinda's brain. Miss Trumble could not object to such a paragon. He certainly looked much older than a man in his twenties, but it was wisdom and experience of life that had shaped him thus, so ran Belinda's thoughts. They would marry, and she would once more be back home in Mannerling with children of her own running across the lawns to the Greek temple by the lake.

Then Lizzie nudged her and said, 'We are going in to supper. You were miles away.'

Belinda smiled slowly. 'I know which gentleman is Lord Saint Clair.'

'Which? Where?'

'Do you see that handsome man at the end of the row in front of us, next to that weak fop? That is he.'

Lizzie's sharp green eyes rested on the tall, handsome figure. 'Are you sure? You cannot know for sure. Besides, he's too old.'

'I know it is he,' said Belinda firmly. 'Come

11

along. I must think of some way to meet him.'

It was a buffet supper. Belinda collected a few dainty items—young ladies were not supposed to eat much—and, forgetting all about Miss Trumble and Lizzie, boldly headed for the end of one of the long tables where the handsome man was just about to sit down.

To her irritation the fop was there before her. But she found a place opposite her quarry and gave him a blinding smile. He answered that smile with a quizzical look and turned to talk to the fop.

Belinda became suddenly aware of Miss Trumble glaring at her across the room. She blushed miserably. She realized in that moment that she had not been introduced to Lord St. Clair, and she could hardly speak to him without a formal introduction.

And then she heard the handsome man say, 'Stop pestering, Saint Clair. I know you are expected to visit the country, but I cannot be of your party.'

Saint Clair? But *he* was Lord St. Clair. Why was he calling the fop St. Clair?

Because, answered the calm voice of returning reason in her head, you made a mistake.

'I have to go to Mannerling,' said Lord St. Clair. 'M'father's furious that I won't even look at the place. You've got to come, Gyre.'

Gyre, thought Belinda. The handsome man

had coached her carefully in the names of all the suitable gentlemen at the London Season.

'What is Mannerling?' asked Lord Gyre.

Belinda bit back an exclamation.

'It's that curst place in the country m'father bought for me,' drawled Lord St. Clair. 'He orders me to marry and live there. Got to find a bride. Get one at this Season and then go to Mannerling and have a huge party, lots of larks.'

'Have you any lady in mind?' asked the marquess.

'No, but anyone will do, provided she's quiet and biddable.'

'Then you'd better get on with it.'

'I am getting on with it,' said Lord St. Clair. 'I'm at this damned musicale being bored out of my wits, aren't I?'

'I thought the music very fine.' Lord Gyre glanced at the beautiful face opposite him, wondering who Belinda was, and also wondering why she was so intently listening to their conversation.

Mrs. Tamworth came up. 'I trust you are enjoying your evening?'

'Very much,' said the marquess. A mocking gleam lit up his eyes. 'Pray, will you not make it perfect by introducing me to this beautiful young lady opposite me?'

With a certain bad grace, Mrs. Tamworth effected the introductions.

'Beverley,' mused Lord St. Clair. His fine

13

hair was so back-combed that it gave him an air of perpetual surprise. 'Oh, I know, you used to own that place, Mannerling.'

'It is the most beautiful place in the world,' said Belinda, her eyes shining.

'Then, pon rep, why did you leave it? Papa in Queer Street?'

'Yes, my lord.'

'Oh, well, I wish you were saddled with it and not I.'

'Did you enjoy the musicale, Miss Beverley?' asked Lord Gyre.

For one moment she hesitated, and then Belinda took the plunge. She gave an affected little laugh and said, 'No, I thought it most horrendous boring.'

Lord St. Clair beamed. 'There you are, Gyre. A soul mate.'

'Obviously,' said the marquess drily. 'What part did you find boring, Miss Beverley? The singing or the piano playing?'

'Both,' said Belinda airily.

'Does anything about the Season amuse you?' he pursued.

Belinda giggled and cast her eyes down, giving both gentlemen a good view of her long black eyelashes. 'I like the balls and parties,' she said, 'and we saw an excellent farce at the playhouse.'

'Was that *The Beau's Revenge?*' asked Lord St. Clair eagerly.

seen it at all, but had read all the very long reviews of it and shrewdly guessed it was just the sort of dismal trite thing to appeal to this fop.

'I say, you are a clever lady. That was the most funniest thing I had ever seen.'

A look of weary distaste crossed Lord Gyre's face. He rose to his feet. 'Excuse me. I see some friends over there.'

'Glad he's gone,' confided Lord St. Clair. 'Stuffed shirt.'

'Then why were you pressing him to go to Mannerling?'

'Oh, Gyre sets the fashion. Bon ton. Can't see it myself. Clothes so drab and plain.'

He twitched the lapels of his buckram-wadded evening coat complacently.

'Mannerling is really such a wonderful place,' said Belinda.

'Oh, let's talk about something else. The thought of living in the country makes me feel ill.'

Miss Trumble watched the pair with a sinking heart. What had happened to all the girl's education, all her intelligence? Oh, Belinda! Simpering and flirting like the most empty-headed of débutantes. Did she not realize that the charade would have to go on for life if she married St. Clair?

What must such as Lord Gyre think of her? Lord Gyre, Miss Trumble knew, was the catch of the Season. I am old and weary, she thought suddenly. Four girls married well. Why should I trouble further? I promised Lizzie I would stay until she was wed. One failure would not matter.

But her heart ached for silly Belinda.

To Belinda's amazement, she did not receive the expected jaw-me-dead from Miss Trumble in the carriage home. That lady fell asleep as soon as the carriage moved off, her ridiculous black wig slipping over one eye. Just in case the governess was feigning sleep, Belinda put a finger to her lips, cautioning Lizzie to silence.

On arrival, they both made hurried good-nights, collected their bed candles from the little table in the hall, and climbed the stairs. Miss Trumble stood and watched them go until their bobbing lights and fluttering muslin skirts had disappeared.

In Belinda's room, Lizzie shut the door behind them and whispered eagerly, 'How did it go? Someone said that ridiculous-looking young man was Lord Saint Clair. And surely that was the one you said was a fop.'

'He is a trifle foppish, I agree,' said Belinda. 'But he is very agreeable.' Belinda was now so determined to secure Lord St. Clair as a husband that she was eager to find virtues in him that did not exist. 'He is very merry and light-hearted.'

'He is young.' Lizzie nodded wisely. 'What if the owner of Mannerling had turned out to be some horrible old man like the one we saw at the church?'

Belinda gave a mock shudder. 'Lord Saint Clair is to be at the rout next evening. Let us hope Mama is well again, for if Miss Trumble comes with us, she will no doubt make sure I do not get a chance to speak to him. Goodness knows,' said Belinda with a world-weary air, 'it is hard enough to talk comfortably to anyone at a London rout.'

'Who was that very handsome man with him?'

'That is the Marquess of Gyre.'

Lizzie sat on the edge of the bed and looked down at her hands. Without looking up, she asked, 'Did you not find him attractive?'

Belinda manufactured a yawn and then said, 'I suppose he is well enough, in his way. Do not be afraid. I am not going to rush off and marry some middle-aged man like my sisters.'

'I should suppose him to be in his thirties.'

'Well, that is middle-aged, as the Good Lord has given us only three score years and ten. Let us not talk about Gyre. Let us talk about Saint Clair. He would make the perfect husband, amiable and not vicious.'

'And he is amusing, witty?'

'Let us say he is the type of gentleman who would be extremely frightened if any female showed the slightest sign of having a brain in her head.'

'I will be devil's advocate,' said Lizzie. 'I will be Miss Trumble. How will such a marriage fare, Belinda, when you find yourself tied to a man with no wit or conversation whatsoever?'

'I will have Mannerling and I will have children, and my lord will be mostly in London. I shall have my own family and my own establishment. I will be able to entertain as we once entertained.'

Lizzie half-closed her green eyes, catlike, as she remembered the splendid balls and parties at Mannerling. Any doubts she had entertained about Lord St. Clair were swept away. She was determined to find him the best of men.

'Did you not think it odd of Miss Trumble to disguise herself so?'

'Miss Trumble is a mystery,' said Belinda. 'But Mama demanded her references and finally got them from her. I gather they were impeccable.'

Lizzie sighed. 'I think there is nothing more sinister in Miss Trumble's past than a broken heart. I think she was jilted and that the man she loved is still on the London scene, no doubt a grandfather by now, and that she does not wish him to see her old and diminished.'

'A very romantical idea.' Belinda laughed. 'I adore our Miss Trumble, but she has always probably been a lowly governess and so she cannot know the passion Mannerling holds for us. *She* has never lived in such a magnificent place.'

'But if her employers were very grand,' said Lizzie doubtfully, 'she would be used to grand households.'

'Being a servant in a grand household is not at all the same thing as being a member of the family,' said Belinda haughtily. She stretched her arms above her head. 'Oh, remember the days of Mannerling, Lizzie. We were *invulnerable.*'

And so both lost themselves in rosy dreams and forgot the rather sterile existence of their early youth when they were wrapped in riches and immense pride.

*   *   *

'And how did the affair go last night?' asked Lady Beverley next day. She was lying on a chaise longue in the drawing-room and the little table beside her was loaded with apothecaries' bottles. Miss Trumble, to whom the question was addressed, often thought that her employer's frequent illnesses were caused by the mixture of medicines she took.

'Well, I think,' said Miss Trumble cautiously, 'Mrs. Tamworth was not, however, pleased that I came in your stead.'

'Then it might teach her to be more careful in her choice of words in future,' said Lady Beverley.

Miss Trumble went and drew back the curtains, finding the darkened room claustrophobic. The sun was shining outside. Down in the street a group of strolling players were dancing to the beat of a tambourine. A fish seller came past, the sunlight gleaming on his basket of mackerel.

'I do not suppose the mysterious Lord Saint Clair was there,' Lady Beverley went on.

'Indeed, he was,' said Miss Trumble mildly.

Lady Beverley sat up. 'And what was he like? Did he meet Belinda?'

'He is an empty-headed fop, vacuous and silly, from my observation.'

'Your observation is not welcome. Remember your place, Miss Trumble.'

'You did ask what he was like,' said Miss Trumble placidly.

'The rout at the Dunsters', tonight. Will he be there?'

'I do not know, my lady.'

'If he has entered the social scene, then he is bound to be there. I am feeling stronger already. I shall escort my girls.'

'Very good, my lady.'

*   *   *

'And,' said Belinda, over her shoulder to Lizzie, as she sat brushing her hair later that day, 'I did hear Lord Saint Clair say to Gyre that he was looking for a wife. He said his father expected him to get married. Don't you see what that means?'

'Yes,' said Lizzie, her eyes shining. 'It means that any compliant lady will do.'

20

'Exactly. Do run along and see if Miss Trumble is to go with us. For if she is, then it will spoil everything, for if I have to act the part of the simpering miss, she will find a way to put a stop to it.'

Lizzie left and returned a few minutes later with the glad news that their mother was to escort them.

'Good,' exclaimed Belinda. 'Now we must think up safe topics of conversation.'

'I gather from Miss Trumble when she is being funny about young misses that gentlemen do not really expect young ladies to have much conversation. The way to a man's heart is through his tailor. You must compliment the cut of his coat.'

Belinda smiled. 'So young and so wise.'

'And you must simper . . . so. You have very long eyelashes, Belinda, and they must be used to advantage.'

Belinda turned and studied her face in the glass. 'My eyebrows are a trifle thin. Many ladies wear false eyebrows these days.'

'Ugh,' said Lizzie with a shudder. 'Those hairy caterpillar things. Even old Lady Dunster wears them, and someone told me at her last ball one slipped and she did not notice until it fell into her glass of champagne. Surely all those false things are for people without your beauty or advantages. You do not need those awful false wax bosoms. Cissy Partridge, you know, the little girl with the bad teeth, had

21

them on last night and she had white-leaded her bosom to hide the join, but they still looked dreadfully false. I told her that she ought to have chosen a gown with a higher neckline and she became quite angry and denied she was wearing anything false.'

Belinda giggled. 'Do you know they even wear false hair . . . down here?' She pointed to her crotch. 'It is advertised in the *Morning Post* '

Lizzie's face turned as red as her hair. Then she rallied. 'You must never talk of such things. What if Lord Saint Clair were to hear you, or any gentleman, for that matter? Oh, sometimes, Belinda, my poor brain feels as if it is cut in half. One half longs for you to marry Saint Clair, but the other guilty half nags me that you are condemning yourself to an empty life and all our excellent education will go unused.'

'Not by my children,' said Belinda. 'That is what Miss Trumble taught us, that a mother with a well-furnished mind is much better for her children than a mother without a single idea in her head.'

Lizzie bit her lip. 'But . . . but if you have a son, your husband will choose a tutor for him, no doubt the sort of tutor he would like himself. The boy will be taught to shoot and hunt and peacock around in fancy clothes and not learn much else.'

Belinda felt a stab of unease. Had she had any idea of what the love between a woman and

22

a man could really be like, she would have had her dreams of Mannerling tempered by dreams of romance. But Mannerling was her sole love and everything else came second to that. The unease fled. She saw herself standing at the head of the staircase at Mannerling, her husband a shadowy figure at her side, receiving guests. In her mind, the sun always shone and the sky was always blue.

Both girls expected a lecture from Miss Trumble before they left for the rout, but that lady was strangely absent. Their sister Abigail, Lady Burfield, did visit them and wished them well and then said, 'Mama is in alt. Evidently you met Saint Clair last night.'

'Yes,' said Belinda airily. 'But there were a great number of interesting gentlemen there as well.'

'Gyre was there?'

'Yes, I was introduced to Lord Gyre.'

'Burfield speaks highly of him,' said Abigail seriously, 'and you are so very beautiful, Belinda. I hope no silly ideas about Mannerling are going to ruin your prospects. Only look how they nearly ruined mine!'

Abigail's own obsession with her old home had brought her to the brink of disgrace and ruin. Her twin, Rachel, was to marry the then owner's son, Harry Devers, but Rachel had panicked before the wedding and so Abigail had taken her place, only to end up panicking herself and fleeing into the arms of Lord

Burfield.

'Harry Devers was a monster,' said Belinda. 'I shall not make the same mistake, Abigail. Be assured,' she went on with a limpid look at her elder sister, 'that Lizzie and I are delighted to be in London and never think of Mannerling at all.'

Abigail looked at her sharply and then gave a satisfied little nod. 'Our Miss Trumble was worried about you.'

'Do you go with us this evening?' asked Lizzie.

Abigail shook her head. 'No, Burfield and I are tired of racketing around. We shall have a quiet evening together at home.'

And Belinda wondered at the calm glow of happiness that emanated from Abigail. How could anyone forget Mannerling so easily?

*   *   *

Lord St. Clair fidgeted as he faced his father, Earl Durbridge. 'So, my boy,' said the earl, 'when are you to take up residence at Mannerling?'

'You want me to find a bride,' said his son patiently, 'and so I am finding one at the Season, which is where one usually finds such a creature.'

'And whom have you found?'

'Early days, Pa,' said Lord St. Clair airily. He waved a scented handkerchief in the air and repeated languidly, 'Early days.'

'Go to it,' growled the earl. 'I am tired of your racketing around. I've a demned good mind to disinherit you and put Peregrine in as my heir.'

'Perry's such a drab little fellow,' expostulated St. Clair. 'I saw him in Saint James's the other day, took one look at his coat, and crossed to the other side of the street.'

The Honourable Peregrine Vane was St. Clair's cousin, a serious young man whose sober ways appealed to the earl immensely.

'He's got a good head on his shoulders,' growled the earl. 'You've done nothing to put Mannerling in order, so I've sent him down there to look the place over.'

'What?' squawked St. Clair. 'That's my place.'

'Then get yourself a bride and show an interest in it.'

Lord St. Clair chewed a fingernail and eyed his father suspiciously. 'You wouldn't really put Perry in my place. Think of the scandal!'

'We'll see,' said the earl. 'Just get a move on and find yourself a bride.'

*   *   *

Routs were probably the most inelegant affairs to be held at the London Season. A rout was not deemed a success unless as many people as possible were crammed into the rooms. It was not the thing to arrive on foot even though one lived only a few streets away. So coachmen fought each other for places and cursed and threatened each other with their long whips.

Then there was the queue to get up the staircase to greet one's hosts before edging into a crowded salon to shout bon mots, carefully rehearsed for days on the part of the gentlemen. As an entertainer with one good popular ballad would take it up and down the country, so the gentleman of fashion, having found one good bon mot, would work it to death in salon after salon, head thrown back, eyes half-closed, witticism delivered at full volume.

As they sweated in buckram-wadded coats, corsets, and high starched collars, the gentlemen envied the ladies the current fashion in thin loose muslin gowns. Since washing all over except for medicinal purposes was only a recent fad, the air was heavy with the smell of perfume, which combined with more evil smells of unwashed bodies and musk from pastilles sucked to counteract the nasty effects of rotting teeth. As she inched to the top of the stairs, Belinda began to feel quite faint and could only marvel that her mother, that dedicated invalid, should appear to feel no ill effects whatsoever.

Then at last she was able to make her curtsy to Lord and Lady Dunster, who sat, throne-like, on two carved chairs to receive their guests. Then it was shuffle and push into the next room, where sweating waiters circulated with iced champagne, easing their bodies eel-like through the press, holding their trays high above their heads.

'I am so thirsty,' mourned Lizzie, 'and I would like a glass of champagne, but how am I to get one. Jump?'

But Belinda had spied Lord St. Clair, and her fine eyes gleamed with the pleasure of the hunt. 'Mama,' she hissed, plucking her mother's sleeve. 'Saint Clair is over there.'

With amazing energy, Lady Beverley propelled her daughters in that direction.

For a brief moment, Belinda found herself jammed up against the Marquess of Gyre, chest-to-chest. She blushed and slid past him. He swivelled to watch her, amazed at the stab of sweet excitement that brief contact had caused.

Lord St. Clair was standing with his bosom friend, Mirabel Dauncey, an equally willowy and foppish creature. 'So I've got to get me a bride,' said Lord St. Clair, stifling a yawn. 'Should I just ask anyone?'

'Won't do,' drawled Mr. Dauncey, raising his quizzing-glass and staring around the company with one huge magnified eye. 'Might get a shrew. Might get some creature who will jaw you to death. Oh, demme. Who's this old fright?'

27

Lady Beverley was smiling in a predatory way as she edged up to them. 'Lord Saint Clair, I believe,' she fluted, extending a thin white-gloved hand like a swan's neck.

'Charmed, madam,' said Lord St. Clair, rolling his eyes at his friend.

'I am Lady Beverley, formerly of Mannerling.'

'I've got that place,' said Lord St. Clair. His pale-blue eyes raked Lady Beverley.

'You are the most fortunate of men,' said Lady Beverley. 'There is no finer house in England.'

'It's in the *country*,' said Lord St. Clair pettishly.

'Yes,' agreed Lady Beverley with undiminished enthusiasm. 'Such lawns, such vistas.'

Belinda saw Lord St. Clair roll his eyes again in the direction of his friend, signalling that he wanted to escape.

She edged forwards until she was standing in front of her mother. 'We met last night, Lord Saint Clair.'

Belinda gave him a dazzling smile. Still Lord St. Clair would have effected his escape had not a dandy drawled somewhere behind him, 'Who is that shiner talking to Saint Clair? Most beautiful creature I've ever seen, demme.'

Saint Clair looked at Belinda with new eyes. He had never until that moment considered asset. 'Of course we did,' he said with a little bow, the crush not permitting a full scrape. Lord Gyre moved close to them.

'I never forget beauty,' Lord St. Clair was saying.

Belinda cast down her long eyelashes, giggled and simpered. 'La, my lord,' she said, 'you do flatter me.'

'I remember we discoursed most intelligently on that rare farce. Better than dull Shakespeare any day, heh, what?'

'Indeed,' gushed Belinda. 'Shakespeare does send me to sleep. I can hardly refrain from yawning.'

Saint Clair looked at her, struck afresh by this kindred spirit. 'Demme, if don't suffer the same ennui. Your honesty is refreshing.'

Again that giggle. 'And compliments from such an arbiter of fashion are always a delight, my lord.'

At that moment, Belinda saw Lord Gyre staring at her, a faint look of contempt in his eyes. Then he turned away. She blushed with mortification, but Lord St. Clair saw that blush and was gratified, thinking he must be possessed of masculine attractions he had hitherto been unaware of.

'I hate these crushes,' he said. 'There is very little opportunity for conversation. May I take you driving tomorrow?'

Lady Beverley smiled graciously. 'Belinda is honoured and charmed to accept your invitation. Come, Belinda.'

Belinda curtsied and moved off with her mother. Her heart was beating hard. But that look the marquess had thrown her was lodged in a corner of her mind and would not go away.

CHAPTER TWO

One had as good be out of the world, as out of the fashion.

—COLLEY CIBBER

The following day Barry asked Lady Beverley's permission to go back to the country. Not only was he given permission but Miss Trumble was ordered to go with him.

'You see,' said Lady Beverley, giving the governess a gracious smile, 'it is not as if the girls need further lessons, and I have various household matters at Brookfield which require your attention.'

Miss Trumble thought quickly. She could stand her ground and point out that she had not been employed as a housekeeper. She knew that Lady Beverley wanted rid of her in case she came between Belinda and Lord St. Clair. Suddenly weary and looking forward to getting out of smoky London, Miss Trumble acquiesced. She was disappointed in Belinda. It was time for the girl to be left to sink or swim. Miss Trumble was heartily sick of the Beverleys

30

and their ongoing schemes and plans to regain Mannerling.

Belinda and Lizzie heard of her imminent departure with mixed feelings. Without their Miss Trumble, the world suddenly seemed an unsafe place. But like their mother, they did not want Miss Trumble to interfere in any of their stratagems. Only Abigail, Lady Burfield, was genuinely upset and went to tell Miss Trumble that if she wished to remain in London, she could resign her employ and stay with the Burfields as their guest for as long as she wished, for life if necessary.

'You are kind,' said Miss Trumble, 'but the air of London does not agree with me.'

'What does not agree with you,' said Abigail shrewdly, 'is that you feel Belinda is out to snare Saint Clair and you have had enough of us silly Beverleys.'

Miss Trumble suddenly smiled. 'Perhaps I could use just a little rest, and perhaps without my constant disapproval, Belinda will see Saint Clair for the empty-headed, useless man he is.'

Abigail was well aware that St. Clair was to take Belinda driving that afternoon and the excitement and flutter that invitation had caused. She gave a little sigh. 'Saint Clair is a fool, but an amiable fool. She could do worse. Burfield hoped that she might attract Gyre. He is intelligent as well as handsome.'

'I think Belinda has ruined herself in Gyre's eyes. I was watching him when she first met

31

Saint Clair and she was simpering and flirting in just the sort of way to put a man like Gyre off. As you say, Saint Clair is weak and shiftless and stupid, but he might make an amiable husband.'

'Are you sure you will not stay?' begged Abigail. 'You were surely instrumental in prompting the rest of us into securing good husbands.'

'I do not know that is the case,' said Miss Trumble seriously. 'I think that with you and your elder sisters, a combination of common sense and love prevailed. Yes, love defeated Mannerling on each count.'

'It is unusual to find love in a society marriage.' Abigail heaved another little sigh. 'Perhaps there will be no great love for Belinda. She will marry Saint Clair, get Mannerling, have children, and settle for that.'

'Mannerling might have other ideas. That is a fickle, evil house.'

'My sensible Miss Trumble! What has happened to you? Mannerling is not a person and does not have feelings.'

'I am not superstitious, and yet . . . and yet there is something about that place—malignancy seems to seep from the very walls. It may take a dislike to Saint Clair.'

Abigail looked at the old governess uneasily. 'I think, dear Miss Trumble, that you have been in contact for too long with the Beverley obsession. It is only a house—bricks and slates and paint. Nothing else.'

*　　　*　　　*

The Honourable Peregrine Vane sat slumped against the squabs in a corner of the travelling-carriage supplied by his uncle, Earl Durbridge, as it turned in at the gates of Mannerling.

He bitterly resented being sent to see the place when that job should be performed by the new owner, Lord St. Clair. Peregrine detested Lord St. Clair. That young man was everything he despised—foppish and empty-headed. In truth Peregrine was bitterly jealous of his cousin, but jealous people are always in competition with the object of their jealousy.

The carriage lurched to a stop. A footman let down the steps. Peregrine climbed wearily down and walked under the porticoed entrance and so into the great hall.

He stood silently for a moment, looking around and then up at the great glittering chandelier and then to the painted ceilings, where gods and goddesses rioted in classic immorality. The air smelled sweetly of wood fires, beeswax, and roses. He felt a great atmosphere of peace and love that seemed to emanate from the very walls.

Feeling strangely like a child coming home from a rather brutal school, he stood drinking in that peace.

'This way, sir,' said a voice at his elbow.

33

He turned to find an elderly housekeeper standing there. The previous housekeeper had been sacked for drunkenness, but that he did not know. This one was grey-haired, motherly, and just as she should be in black bombazine gown and starched white cap with a ring of keys clinking at her waist. 'I am Mrs. Muir, sir,' she said. 'The servants have taken your bags to your room.'

Peregrine smiled. Although he was a fairly handsome man with square regular features and a neat figure, he did not often smile. 'I think I would like some refreshment first if I may,' he said.

'Very well, sir. The day is chilly and there is a fire in the Green Saloon.'

He followed her up the stairs. A chain of saloons lay on the first floor, where in the grand days of Mannerling balls had been held. The Green Saloon was large and magnificent. A bright fire crackled in the hearth. Peregrine walked to the fire and said over his shoulder, 'Some claret, I think.'

When the housekeeper had left, he studied his reflection in the glass over the fireplace. It seemed to him that he had grown in stature. He sank down in a comfortable armchair by the fire and stared dreamily into the flames. A footman appeared shortly with a glass, a decanter of claret, and some thin ham sandwiches on a tray.

The claret was excellent and the ham was

Westphalian. Peregrine stretched out his booted legs.

But gradually as he drank and stared about him, the feeling of peace began to leave him. This should be mine, he thought furiously. Why should a churl, a man-milliner like Toby St. Clair, have all this when he does not even want it?

And then he began to remember remarks Earl Durbridge had made. 'I've a good mind to disinherit that boy, Perry. Yes, any more of his japes and roistering and I will do just that. But Mannerling and marriage will settle him, you'll see.'

'Yes, we shall most certainly see about that,' said Peregrine aloud. He grinned at the leaping flames in the fireplace and the flames illuminated that face.

'Gave me quite a turn,' said the housekeeper, Mrs. Muir, in the servants' hall later that day, for she had entered and had stopped short in the doorway, seeing that evil grin. 'Looked like a soul in hell, that Mr. Vane did. But it was a trick of the light, and we all know this place do play strange tricks on the imagination.'

*   *   *

While Peregrine plotted his cousin's downfall, Lord St. Clair was driving Belinda in the park and enjoying immensely the admiring stares

35

her beauty was drawing towards his carriage. Why, even his best swansdown waistcoat had failed to get all this attention! Belinda smiled and nodded to various people she had already met at balls and parties, all the while hanging tightly on to the guard rail and bracing her feet against the spatter-board, for St. Clair was driving a showy team with a propensity to rear and back. St. Clair was impervious to the fact that his driving was awful. Lord Gyre came darting past in a phaeton with a pretty lady next to him. He alone did not slow to view the charms of Belinda.

Fortunately for Belinda's equanimity, St. Clair's horses grew weary of shying and bucking and backing and made up their minds to head homewards at a sedate pace. After a few futile efforts to dissuade them, St. Clair decided to let them have their own way and look as if it were all his own idea. The easy pace at last made conversation possible.

'May I say, Miss Belinda,' he remarked, 'that your bonnet is vastly fetching?'

'Oh, my lord,' fluttered Belinda, 'I put it on especially for you.'

The bonnet was her sister Abigail's. It was a little straw hat with a high crown tilted at a rakish angle to show her shiny black curls.

'Do you go to the opera tonight?' asked Belinda.

'I can't stand all that caterwauling and it's Mozart again and that fellow gives me a pain in the head.'

'So monstrous boring,' agreed Belinda. 'But one goes to be seen and your fashion and style are so much admired.'

'Hey, you are right. Only cloth-heads bother about the music and one can sit in the back of the box and have a comfortable coze. Then there's the opera ball afterwards. Got a box?'

'Yes, my brother-in-law, Burfield, has one.'

'Then I'll join you.'

Belinda's world lurched a little. She loved the opera, loved the music, and the idea of talking all through it horrified her. But there was Mannerling. And look at the freedom married ladies had. Many of them went to the opera with friends rather than with husbands.

'I'll call for you,' went on St. Clair. He had not waited to see if she wanted his escort. Secure in his own vanity, he could not contemplate anything other than that she should be honoured and delighted.

And so the evening was quite a nightmare for Belinda. As Lord St. Clair chattered on at the back of the opera box, several angry voices kept calling on him to be quiet. There was to be further mortification. Lord St. Clair was handed a note. He crackled it open and read the contents and then gave an angry snort. 'Would you believe this, Miss Belinda,' he said in a loud carrying voice. 'Gyre says if I don't shut up, he'll call me out!'

Saint Clair stood up and walked to the edge

of the box, raised his quizzing-glass and glared all around in what he considered was a threatening way. But the recollection that Gyre was reputed to be the best shot and swordsman in the country made him finally sit down and fall into a sulky silence.

Gratefully, Belinda gave herself up to the beauty of the music.

At the opera ball afterwards, as he promenaded with Belinda after a set of the quadrille, he said, 'Tedious, was it not? I thought you had gone to sleep.'

Belinda gave a silly giggle. 'So boring and long. I declare I nearly did. But, la, my lord, how could I sleep with you to keep me company?'

'I must warn you, my fair charmer, I'm a devil with the ladies.'

'Oh, my lord, do you mean you are enamoured of someone? I declare you break my poor heart.'

'Hey, only bamming. No one else here to match you.'

After the promenade was over, Belinda slipped away. She wanted a few moments by herself because her resolve to marry St. Clair was slipping. She went to a dressing-room set aside for the ladies and sat down in a chair in front of the mirror and gazed wearily at her own reflection. Somehow, without the disapproving Miss Trumble around to react to, the idea of securing such a fool for a husband

38

was beginning to strike Belinda as ridiculous. She pinned up a stray curl, shook out her muslin skirts, and made to leave the room. The door of the dressing-room was open. She heard the Marquess of Gyre's voice and shrank back. The marquess made her feel as if she were perpetually making a cake of herself. 'Which is exactly what you are doing, Belinda,' said Miss Trumble's voice in her head.

'You must admit, Gyre,' said his companion's voice, 'that the Beverley girl—Belinda, is it?—is the most beautiful creature in London.'

Then came the marquess's voice with dreadful clarity, 'Oh, she is well enough, I suppose, but so stupid and vain.' His voice rose to a falsetto as he began to parody Belinda, 'Oh, my lord, opera is so tedious and boring, the finest works of art are so boring. La, your waistcoat is the very height of fashion.'

'Was that meant to be Belinda Beverley? Doesn't sound like her. Got a pretty voice.'

'But the content was hers,' said Gyre drily. 'They all talk like that.'

'Which is why I am still unwed,' said the marquess. 'Someone told me the Beverley girls were highly educated. Perhaps because they are able to spell "cat" without looking up Doctor Johnson's dictionary.'

'Well, you know,' said his companion, sounding amused, 'if she is behaving like a silly widgeon, it's all part of the plot.'

'You interest me—go on.'

'It is a well-known fact that the Beverleys have thought of little but getting their family home back again. They lost all when old Beverley spent all his money, house and lands, across the tables of Saint James's. Do you not remember the scandal when Rachel Beverley was set to marry the owner of Mannerling, Harry Devers, got cold feet and so her place at the wedding was taken by her twin Abigail? Abigail decides she cannot go through with it after the farce of a marriage and to escape Devers, jumps into Burfield's bed. You'll probably find that Belinda Beverley is really as sharp as a whip and that if Saint Clair did not have Mannerling, she would not give him the time of day.'

'What a disgusting little creature,' remarked Lord Gyre. 'Shall we face the music again or go to the club?'

'I think another few dances.'

They moved off. Belinda retreated back into the dressing-room, her face flaming. Why should she have thought that all the Beverley scandals had been forgotten? If Lord St. Clair did not know of them, he soon would. Some competitive society mother would soon find a way to put him wise.

Belinda clenched her little fists. 'Damn Mannerling,' she said aloud.

In the refreshment room, Lord St. Clair was hearing all about the history of the Beverleys

40

from his friend, Mirabel Dauncey.

'So you see what I mean, old fellow,' said Mirabel at the end of a catalogue of Beverley iniquities, 'she only wants that demned house, not you.'

Lord St. Clair's amour propre was severely dented.

'I'll keep clear of her,' he said. 'That'll show her.'

* * *

It was a silent carriage ride home. Lord St. Clair had sent an opera servant with a note to say he could not escort Lady Beverley, Belinda, and Lizzie home. He had the headache. It was a dreadful snub. After wondering aloud and plaintively what could have possibly happened to disaffect him, Lady Beverley had fallen into a miserable silence.

When they arrived back, Lizzie would have followed Belinda to her room, but Belinda said, 'Not tonight, Lizzie. I am too depressed and too tired.'

Belinda lay awake for a long time, writhing with mortification. How could she have been so silly? When Lord St. Clair next called, she would drop her act and be herself again.

* * *

But a week passed and Lord St. Clair did not call. But he thought of Belinda often, not in any

41

amorous way, but he regretted losing this important fashion accessory. He remembered all the admiring stares in the park. No one had given him an admiring stare since then. Not even his new bottle-green coat with the wide lapels and high buckram-wadded shoulders and silver buttons had drawn so much as a glance.

But still he would not have approached Belinda again had not matters taken a dangerous turn.

He was summoned again by his father.

'As you know, I sent Perry to Mannerling to make sure everything was running smoothly,' said the earl, waving a letter in his son's delicately painted face. 'He has done a marvellous job and has come up with some excellent plans for the place. Perhaps I should let him have the estate.'

Lord St. Clair went a trifle pale under his paint. 'Can't do that, Pa. I'm your heir.'

'I don't think you will be for much longer, m'boy. You seem to have done nothing about finding a bride. I heard you were seen with that shiner, Belinda Beverley.'

Lord St. Clair's not usually agile brain suddenly began to work ferociously. He was about to tell his father all about the scheming Beverleys, but his father would then think him even more of a fool. After all, Belinda Beverley was admired. Married to her, he could point out she had gained what she wanted—

Mannerling—and then go cheerfully on his own hedonistic way.

'As a matter of fact,' said Lord St. Clair, 'that was something I meant to put to you. Belinda Beverley is all that is suitable and her family used to have Mannerling before old Beverley went to Queer Street and lost everything. She'll know all the tenants and useful things like that and all the local county. Thought of going to Mannerling in a couple of weeks' time and inviting the fair Belinda and her mother down. Little house party. Can't woo with Perry around, so tell him to quit the place sharpish.'

The earl looked at his son in amazement. 'Well, I declare, you have some of the right stuff in you after all! Go to it, m'boy. You have my blessing.'

'Thank you, Pa,' said his son meekly. 'But get rid of Perry!'

*　　　*　　　*

Barry Wort had heard reports of what was going on at Mannerling. One morning, shortly after he and Miss Trumble had arrived back at Brookfield House, he said, 'I gather he's the Honourable Peregrine Vane.'

'Have you heard good reports of him?' asked Miss Trumble. They were standing by the cabbage plot and she drew her shawl more closely about her shoulders, for the day was cold with an irritating, blustery wind.

'The servants do say he might end up the owner of Mannerling after all. The gossip runs that Earl Durbridge favours this Mr. Vane as a sensible fellow while sometimes despairing of his son. I have heard no bad reports of Mr. Vane.'

'I confess I am curious, Barry. Perhaps Mr. Vane would be a more suitable parti for Belinda. I wish I could think of some reason for calling.'

Barry leaned on his spade and furrowed his brow. At last his face cleared. 'You could say that Lady Beverley left a shawl there when she last called.'

Miss Trumble laughed. 'Excellent. We shall go to Mannerling this afternoon, Barry.'

*　　　*　　　*

That afternoon Perry, on receiving the intelligence that the Beverleys' governess had called, was about to tell the footman to inform Miss Trumble that he was not at home. But he had gone to great pains to ingratiate himself with the servants and tenants and so decided it would be politic to receive her.

He smiled graciously at the elderly governess when she was ushered in, but was a little taken aback at the modishness of her gown and the grandeur of her manner.

'You are most gracious to receive me, sir,' said Miss Trumble. 'Lady Beverley left a red-

44

and-gold wool shawl the last time she was here and wondered if it had been found.'

Perry pulled the green-and-gold embroidered bell-pull and told a footman who promptly answered its summons to bring in tea and cakes and then question the staff about the whereabouts of the shawl.

Perry had always made a point of listening to servants' gossip and so he had heard all about the ambitions of the Beverleys. He could not blame them for such ambitions, for sometimes he felt he could cheerfully kill to make Mannerling his own. In all his selfish life, he had never known a love like this. Before dinner, he would stroll about the lawns and smoke a cigar and drink in the great enfolding peace of the place.

'Perhaps you can help me, Miss Trumble,' he said, after the tea-tray had been brought in.

'I will be glad to help you in any way I can,' said Miss Trumble, thinking what a sensible and reliable young man he was.

'I have been thinking,' said Perry, 'that it is about time I got to know some of the local county. What do you suggest? A fête? A ball? Start off with a turtle supper?'

Miss Trumble concealed her surprise. Then she said tentatively, 'I will be glad to supply you with the names of your neighbours, those that are suitable. Are you acting on behalf of Lord Saint Clair?'

'I doubt if we shall be seeing him,' he said

smoothly. 'Earl Durbridge, my uncle, has put me in charge. I plan to be here for some time.'

'Indeed, sir. Then, if you will supply me with pen and paper, I will make you out a list.'

He ushered her over to a writing-desk by the window, opened the lid, and stood behind her when she sat down at it, rubbing his hands. 'Now, I want you, Miss . . .?'

'Trumble.'

'Trumble. I want you to put opposite each name a thumbnail sketch, and some idea of rank. People without titles can be of the first stare, you know.'

'I know,' said Miss Trumble, beginning to write.

'What is it, Henry?' she heard him ask, and then a footman replying, 'This express has just come for you, sir. And, sir, no one has found such a shawl as Miss Trumble says that Lady Beverley left.'

'Oh, give it here. Keep on writing, Miss Tremble.'

'Trumble.'

She heard him crackle open the seal. Then she heard him draw in his breath in a sharp hiss. She swung round in her chair and looked up at him. His face was a mask of baffled fury.

'Not bad news, I trust?' she asked.

'What, no! None of your business. Be off with you. I have matters to attend to here.'

Miss Trumble rose and curtsied.

The footman held open the double doors of

the saloon and then closed them behind her. Miss Trumble paused on the landing, making a great business of pulling on her gloves in case any servant should see her.

'I shall be leaving tomorrow,' she heard Perry say in a thin voice. 'You are to make Mannerling ready for Lord Saint Clair.'

'When does he arrive, sir?'

'In a mere week's time, with guests, and one of them is his intended bride, Belinda Beverley.'

'Very good, sir.'

'That's one of those damned Beverleys who have always been plotting and scheming to get this place back.' Perry promptly forgot that only a short time ago he had been in sympathy with the Beverleys' ambitions. 'Demme, that was the Beverley governess that was just here. And I entertained her! Pah! I'll scotch their schemes.'

'Very good, sir.'

'And don't you go blabbing any of this in the servants' hall, mind.'

'No, sir, I am the soul of discretion.'

'See that you are. What a wretched coil. I never thought Toby Saint Clair would comply with his father's wishes. He'll run Mannerling into the ground; you'll see.'

The voices suddenly came nearer the door. Miss Trumble sped lightly down the stairs.

'So that is that,' she said to Barry as he drove her homewards. 'As I see it, this Mr. Vane

47

wants Mannerling for himself. Oh, my poor Belinda. But if Saint Clair is bringing Belinda here and Mr. Vane is absent, there is little he can do.'

* * *

Belinda could not know the plans to invite her to Mannerling because so far Lord St. Clair had forgotten to tell her or make a point of seeing her. First there was a prize-fight on the Sussex Downs and then the roistering that followed afterwards to keep him out of town. Nor had he thought whom else to invite to the country.

Long experience had trained him to say he would do something to please his father and then, when the threat of disinheritance had disappeared, to promptly forget what it was he had promised.

So Belinda attended balls, parties, routs, and the opera, relieved that she had no longer to play the part of a silly miss. To her mother's distress, she began to disaffect suitors by her 'masculine' conversation, for Belinda was interested in military and political matters in a way that no young lady should be. As it also got about that she had little dowry to speak of, she lost any attractions she might have had for a gentleman who was prepared to overlook the handicap of intelligence in a future bride for the sake of money.

Belinda appeared deaf to criticism, and her sister Abigail, who had luckily married a highly intelligent man, was of no help at all, or so Lady Beverley constantly moaned. She blamed Miss Trumble for this unmaidenly curse of superior education that had been inflicted on Belinda.

Belinda did not even seem to have a proper fear of spinsterhood. A woman who did not marry might just as well not exist. She could perhaps make herself useful in the family, taking over some of the role of unpaid housekeeper. Had she money, she might become a fashionable eccentric. But without it, she might be condemned to the life of a governess.

Love did not normally enter into marriage among the upper classes. Marriage was a business arrangement. When a woman married, her husband was her absolute master, with total rights over the children. If they separated, though it might be his fault, she was totally dependent on him for access to her children.

Fear of being left on the shelf drove the terrified débutantes into preening and flirting, giggling, talking baby talk and bad French. Behind each débutante was a powerful family who expected the horrendous expense of a Season to be paid back in full by an advantageous marriage.

Belinda, however, was being brought out by

a rich and indulgent elder sister who had married for love. Abigail's husband had made Lady Beverley a generous present of money so that her daughter could boast a fine dowry. But the miserly Lady Beverley had squirrelled the money away for her own use. For had not four of her daughters married well with only modest dowries? Money was not to be wasted when beauty could bring the same result.

Abigail was in blissful ignorance of this state of affairs, and being too high-minded to gossip was not aware that society believed Belinda to be badly dowered.

And so, at a very grand ball, even little Lizzie was startled to see that Belinda was actually having to sit out during a waltz at which she, Lizzie, being partnered by a jolly young captain, was taking the floor. Lizzie was not aware of her own popularity. Lady Beverley had dinned into her from an early age that her looks were 'unfortunate.'

Lord Gyre noticed the phenomenon of dance-less Belinda as well. He turned to his friend, Gurney Burke. 'The Beverley charmer does not seem to be taking this Season. What can have gone wrong with our simpering miss?'

'I have heard that Miss Belinda has a sharp brain and likes to talk of politics, women's rights, and military matters,' remarked Gurney, a plump, easy-going gentleman.

'You amaze me. I thought her the most empty-headed simpering miss I had ever come across. But then, I also heard of the Beverleys' ambitions to regain Mannerling, their old home. So perhaps Miss Belinda was only simpering and ogling to ensnare Saint Clair.' He studied Belinda curiously. He noticed that she did not have the disconsolate look of most wallflowers. She sat calmly, the many flounces of her muslin gown cascading to her small feet. She had a little smile on her mouth as she watched her sister.

She intrigued him. He would try to secure her for the supper dance and see which face she presented to him.

To his surprise, when he bowed before her and asked her to dance, a little flash of dislike darted like a fish at the back of her beautiful eyes before they became a polite blank. Belinda did not want to dance with this man who had mocked her. But, she thought rapidly, if she refused him then the laws of society decreed that she would not be able to dance with anyone else and she would have to join her mother at the supper-table and listen to her seemingly endless list of complaints and disappointments. After what seemed to him an unconscionable length of time, although in fact it was only a few moments, Belinda rose and curtsied and allowed him to lead her into the set of a country dance.

She danced beautifully but did not try to converse. At the end of the dance, he held out his arm. She placed her gloved fingertips delicately on it and he led her into the supper-room.

On the way in, Belinda nodded or exchanged greetings with acquaintances. Finally, when they were seated and food and wine had been served to them, he said, 'Are you still bored by the Season, Miss Beverley?'

She regarded him coolly. 'I am not so much bored, my lord, as bewildered and depressed.'

'Indeed! Why?'

'It is like being part of a pretty auction with myself as one of the cows, waiting for a bidder.'

'You mean you feel you must find a husband?'

Her beautiful mouth curled in a mocking smile. 'Why not? This is what all this charade is about.'

'I do not like the picture of the cattle market. Inelegant.'

'Then perhaps we are like elaborately dressed dolls on the toy-shop shelf waiting for a buyer.'

'I was not aware you were a cynic.'

'Believe me, sir, I am all things that are unfashionable. One of them is that I have a very healthy appetite.'

'And I am stopping you eating by my questions? Fall to, Miss Beverley. I shall not disturb you until you are chopped and watered.'

With mixed feelings of pique and amusement, he watched the fair Belinda settle down to enjoy her food.

At last he said, 'May I speak now?'

'If you wish.'

'Are you usually so blunt?'

'Not always. If I am hunting, I can be quite empty-headed and frivolous.'

'Then I should be relieved that I am obviously not one of your quarries. But why? I am titled and rich and not deformed.'

'You do not have the necessary requirement, my lord.'

His strange eyes flashed with anger. 'The necessary requirement being Mannerling.'

'Ah, you have heard all the old Beverley scandals,' she said lightly. 'Who has not? And you are shocked and disgusted at such unmaidenly behaviour. Think of your own house and lands, my lord. If both were taken from you, would you not do everything in your power to reclaim them?'

'Of course. But I am a man.'

Belinda regarded him seriously. 'Think of what you have just said. Does it not strike you as ridiculous? I confess when I go to the play to have much sympathy with old Shylock. When he begins his famous speech, 'When you prick us, do we not bleed?' he is saying, 'Am I not a human being with human feelings just like you?'

He gave a reluctant laugh. 'You must admit that masculine ambition does not sit well on beauty.'

'No, I will not admit it. Women have every right to be as ambitious as men. But men are never thwarted so much in their ambitions. Women cannot join the army or navy, fight for their country, take a profession—they cannot even find work as a stay-maker. So what is left? Governess or seamstress; shop work, but only in a confectioner's; inn skivvy—badly paid, degrading work.'

'You invite me to be as blunt as you. How can women take any masculine jobs when their function in life is to bear children?'

'Once a year, until they die. Women should be allowed a choice—profession or motherhood.'

'It is no use kicking against the pricks, Miss Beverley. That state of affairs will never happen.'

'So do you also consider education for women a waste of time, my lord?'

'Gently born ladies are always educated, Miss Belinda.'

'You pretend not to know what I mean. I am talking about education in the so-called masculine sciences, chemistry and mathematics.'

'And you have been educated in such?'

'Thoroughly, my lord. We have an excellent governess.'

'And a most unusual one. You are fortunate.'

'You approve!'

'Oh, yes, beauty such as yours combined with

54

a well-informed mind is enchanting.'

Belinda made a disappointed moue. 'Ah, you are flirting. But I am all out of blushes and simpers tonight, my lord. And here is this magnificent pudding lying in front of me, as yet untouched.'

'Go to it! More wine?'

'A glass of water, if you please, my lord.'

He waved to a waiter and asked him to fetch a pitcher of water and two glasses.

'You do not eat your pudding, my lord?'

'I do not like sweet things, Miss Beverley, and that includes silly débutantes, one of which you have hitherto given an excellent imitation of. Was that to ensnare Saint Clair?'

Afterwards, Belinda was to wonder miserably if she had run mad. But for the heady moment, she was enjoying being truthful. She smiled at him and he felt his heart give a treacherous lurch. 'Of course.'

'Now, Miss Beverley, let us be sensible. I like Saint Clair because he is harmless and without vice. But what is the charm of this house, this Mannerling, that can cause you to contemplate having to play such a role for the rest of your life?'

'It is a role I would have to play only until such time as I was married, my lord.'

'And love does not enter into your speculations?'

'No, my lord. My elder sisters are fortunate, I suppose, but I can find nothing of that gentler

55

emotion in me. I think I would love my children and educate them well.'

'But your frivolous husband, supposing it were Saint Clair, might have other ideas. We, in society, do not love our children.' A trace of bitterness crept into his voice. 'They are often sent out to foster-mothers and then returned to the nursery, only to see their parents on high days and holidays, when they are presented before them in their best clothes for a few moments. For a boy there is a tutor, then school, and then the army.'

'Such having been your own experience?'

'Such having been every boy's experience, Miss Beverley. Give up your pursuit of Saint Clair, and try to find someone a trifle more intelligent. There are such men.'

'Alas, Saint Clair has given up his pursuit of me.'

'Which all goes to show his lack of worth. Shall we return to the ballroom?'

Belinda felt a stab of caution. 'My lord, I must beg of you not to repeat any of our conversation. I do not know what came over me this evening.'

'I shall not talk about it, Miss Beverley, but I shall remember every word of it with pleasure.'

She looked at him doubtfully from under her long eye-lashes. 'Come, you have my promise,' he said.

Belinda was crowded by men vying to dance with her for the rest of the evening. She had forgotten that Lord Gyre set the fashion. As soon as she had left him, Gurney Burke was at the marquess's elbow. 'Well, how did you find the farouche Miss Belinda?'

Lord Gyre deliberately raised his voice so that it carried to many listening ears. 'Not farouche at all. I found her intriguing and enchanting. Miss Belinda Beverley will set the fashion for intelligent young ladies.'

And so it was that society decided that Belinda was to be courted or, in the case of the ladies, emulated.

But tired Belinda, falling into bed that night, could only think that she had made a fool of herself and supplied the formidable Lord Gyre with further ammunition to despise her.

*   *   *

Society news travels fast, and so it was that Lord St. Clair in Brighton quickly heard that the Marquess of Gyre was to all accounts smitten with Belinda Beverley. His promise to his father came roaring back into his head and, alarmed, he drove at a breakneck pace for London. He sweated through what he considered a truly awful evening at the opera without seeing Belinda. The next day, he dressed in his best and went to call. He was informed by Abigail that Belinda, Lizzie, and her mother were out on calls.

To Abigail's surprise, he insisted on waiting

for them. After half an hour of the most vacuous conversation poor Abigail felt it had ever been her ill luck to endure, she gratefully heard them return.

Lord St. Clair stood up, suddenly nervous. Belinda came in followed by Lady Beverley. Lizzie had gone to her room.

Lady Beverley had been feeling tired and cross. The fact that various London hostesses envied her for Lord Gyre's approval of Belinda had passed her by. On the road home she had returned to her usual berating of Belinda for having disaffected Lord St. Clair.

But the knowledge that that young man had actually called had worked like champagne on her spirits. 'Why, my lord,' she cried. 'We are deeply honoured.'

Saint Clair bowed. 'I am come,' he said, tugging at his cravat, 'to invite you, Lady Beverley, and your daughters, to a little house party at Mannerling.'

'Charmed,' said Lady Beverley, feeling quite faint with gratitude.

'Perhaps we could leave next week, ma'am?'

'I am sure we could manage that,' said Lady Beverley eagerly. 'We have so many invitations to cancel, of course, because Belinda is all the crack.'

But Lord St. Clair was looking anxiously at Belinda. 'Miss Belinda? My invitation pleases you?'

Somewhere inside Belinda's mind a prison

door slammed shut. She cast down her eyelashes and giggled. 'I am overwhelmed at the honour, my lord.'

Finding out which function they were to attend that evening, Lord St. Clair promised to be there and bowed his way out.

Lady Beverley hugged her daughter. 'Mannerling is as good as ours, my precious,' she cried.

* * *

'So you've done it,' said Mirabel Dauncey. 'Couldn't you find anyone other than a Beverley?'

'Has its advantages,' said St. Clair. 'I mean, everyone notices her and envies me. Besides, she'll know all these boring things like servants and tenants.'

'You know,' said Mirabel cautiously, 'it's going the rounds that Belinda Beverley is a bit too intelligent for her own good. Being damned as a bit of a bluestocking.'

Saint Clair sighed and waved a scented handkerchief in the air with one languid white hand. 'That's the other reason she fancies me,' he said with simple vanity. 'Got a good brain, me.'

'Have you put that good brain to use and invited other people?' said Mirabel. 'I mean, if you go off the chit, you can always protest she was just one of the crowd.'

59

'I'll round up a few people,' said St. Clair sulkily.

'Tell you what,' said Mirabel. 'I'll do it for you.'

'Would you? I say, that's uncommon kind of you.'

'I'm your best friend, ain't I?'

* † *

But Mirabel had an ulterior motive. He often thought St. Clair was too naïve, too innocent, not a downy one like himself. Also, St. Clair was lazy. Belinda Beverley was the easiest and—because of Mannerling—guaranteed not to turn him down. But Mirabel had heard the rumours about Belinda's lack of dowry. Money should marry money. It was the way of the world. Now there was Miss Jane Chalmers, very rich and quite neat-looking. She was being brought out by her widowed mother. Time to get dressed and make a call there. Then what about Gyre? People said it had obviously amused the marquess to favour Belinda. He was an attractive, rich man. That might put a spoke in the wheel. It would be difficult enough prying people away from the London Season. Hopeful young ladies would be easy enough.

He set out on his rounds.

* * *

Mirabel found it all much easier than he

expected. To his surprise and relief, not only Lord Gyre but his friend, Gurney Burke, agreed to accept the invitation. Jane Chalmers and her mother also said they would come. He then asked the fashionable and dazzling Mrs. Ingram, reputed to have been once Gyre's mistress, and two débutantes, the Hartley twins, Margaret and Polly, and their parents. His hope in asking Mrs. Ingram was that she might rouse a spark of jealousy in Belinda's bosom and ignite her interest in Gyre.

Quite carried away by his success in this new role as entrepreneur, Mirabel then urged St. Clair to travel to Mannerling ahead of the guests to oversee all the arrangements for their visit.

*   *   *

Earl Durbridge looked fondly at his nephew, the Honourable Peregrine Vane, on the day the house party was due to begin, and said, 'It did the trick sending you to Mannerling, Perry, m'boy. Brought that scapegrace son of mine to heel.'

Perry smiled blandly to cover up his raging feelings. Then he said, 'I was a bit alarmed to find out that Toby's intended is Miss Belinda Beverley.'

'How so? What's up with the girl?'

So Perry, in a calm, level voice told him all about the past machinations of the Beverleys to regain Mannerling and waited gleefully for the expected wrathful and horrified reaction of the earl.

But it was the earl who appeared oddly calm. 'Do you think I don't know all about the Beverleys? I found out as much about that family as I could. The elder girls have made good marriages, away from Mannerling. And if this Belinda's interest is in getting Mannerling, then well and good, and I'll tell you why. No other female has seemed particularly struck with my poor Toby. He cares more for his dress than any female. But I want grandsons. This Belinda is in prime health, and a beauty. She'll make fine children. She knows Mannerling and the neighbourhood. If she's strong-willed enough to take on Toby, then she'll be strong-willed enough to make a man of him. You're never going to turn mawkish and tell me she doesn't love him. Who loves who in this wicked world of society marriages, hey?'

'But Mannerling itself is a jewel,' said Perry desperately. 'Toby will offend the tenantry and the county with his wild ways, his profligate ways, and he will run the estates into the ground.'

'That's where a strong wife will come in. Tell you what, Perry, and I say this because you are a good-hearted boy. Get back down there and join that house party and tell Toby I sent you. Keep an eye on things and report back to me.'

'I will gladly do that,' said Perry. 'My only

desire is to do your wishes.'

The earl's normally hard face softened. 'You're a Trojan, Perry. Between us, we will see that lad of mine safely wed.'

Over my dead body, Perry thought.

*　　　*　　　*

When the Beverley carriage turned in at the gates of Mannerling, Lizzie was beside herself with excitement. 'We are going home,' she said over and over again.

Belinda tried to feel some elation but could not. All she could think of was how soon she would be able to see Miss Trumble again. Everyone was so pleased with her; even her sister Abigail had viewed the possible betrothal to St. Clair with complacence. 'I always thought of you as the quiet, romantic one,' Abigail had said. 'But it looks as if you are the most pragmatic of all of us.'

Belinda felt that if only Miss Trumble would appear to tell her she was throwing her life away for the sake of Mannerling, she could react to the criticism and find all the courage and determination she had lost. She would not admit to herself that courage and determination had faded—not when she thought St. Clair had lost interest in her, but when she had taken supper with Lord Gyre.

The carriage stopped outside the porticoed entrance. Lady Beverley, Lizzie, and Belinda

63

entered in a flurry of maids and footmen. There was a new butler, very correct and stately, and Mrs. Muir, the housekeeper, whose efficiency had so pleased Perry.

To Belinda's relief and Lady Beverley's obvious disappointment, the butler, called Jiggs, informed them that the master was unwell. Saint Clair had indulged in a drinking competition with his friend Mirabel the night before and was suffering from the effects.

Lady Beverley heard the sound of female laughter and frowned. 'We have other guests, Jiggs?' she demanded, forgetting that she was a guest at Mannerling and not its mistress.

'Most of the other guests are arrived, my lady,' said Jiggs as he led the way up the double staircase under the painted ceilings. The chandelier sent out a merry tinkling sound although there was no wind—the chandelier on which Judd, one of the previous owners, had hanged himself. Lizzie gave it a nervous look. 'Why is the chandelier moving, Jiggs?'

The butler glanced at the chandelier and said, 'It sometimes does that, miss, and to tell you the truth, we have never been able to find out why. In fact, the servants this very day are putting steel cords on either side, to moor it, so to speak, miss.'

'Who are these other guests?' fretted Lady Beverley.

'Mrs. Chalmers and her daughter; Mrs. Ingram; Mr. and Mrs. Hartley and their twin daughters; Lord Saint Clair's friend, Mr. Dauncey; his cousin, Mr. Vane; Lord Gyre; and Mr. Burke.'

'Gyre . . . here?' demanded Lady Beverley.

'We are indeed honoured to have the marquess's presence,' said Jiggs smoothly.

As soon as they were in their rooms, Lizzie scampered along to Belinda's and said, 'So Gyre is here? Do not tell me history is going to repeat itself and you are going to throw away Mannerling for Gyre?'

Belinda coloured slightly but said in an even voice, 'Do not nag me, Lizzie. We are home, are we not? But there are other ladies here . . . competition.'

'Nobody can compete with you, Belinda.'

'I have heard of this Miss Jane Chalmers,' said Belinda. 'She is very, very rich.'

'Pooh! So is Saint Clair.'

'All the more reason for him to marry money. The Hartley twins, Margaret and Polly, are frivolous and also rich. Does Mannerling still mean so very much to you, Lizzie?'

'Of course it does, and to you, too.'

Belinda walked to the window and stared down, willing her old home to exert its usual magic on her, but she felt nothing. Then she saw the little carriage from Brookfield House coming up the drive, driven by Barry. And sitting bolt upright in it was Miss Trumble.

'Miss Trumble is come!' cried Belinda, and without waiting for Lizzie, she shot out of the room.

Lizzie stayed where she was. For once in her life she wished Miss Trumble would stay away. What if Miss Trumble talked Belinda out of her ambitions?

Miss Trumble smiled as the little carriage came to a halt and Belinda erupted out of the house, her skirts flying. But she said severely, 'Ladies do not run, Belinda.'

Unabashed, Belinda smiled. 'Only when they see you. Come with me and take tea. We shall have it in my private sitting-room. They have given me the Yellow Room. I would have liked my old rooms but visitors can't be choosers. Barry! Are you well?'

'Fair to middling, Miss Belinda,' said the odd man. 'Bit of stiffness in the joints.'

'Take the carriage to the stables, Barry,' said Miss Trumble. 'I heard you were come, Belinda, with other guests.'

'Yes, other guests,' agreed Belinda, linking her arm in the governess's. 'Pretty girls, and rich, too! What of my chances?'

'Shh. The servants will hear you.'

Once they were in Belinda's sitting-room and tea had been served, Miss Trumble said, 'Do you think Saint Clair means to propose to you?'

'Yes, I do,' said Belinda. 'I may of course be terribly mistaken. He may just be shopping for a bride and so has asked those he considers suitable.'

She waited expectantly for Miss Trumble to lecture her on her folly, but the governess took a delicate sip of tea and said, 'Who are the other guests? Tell me about them.'

Belinda listed the guests, ending up with the name of Lord Gyre.

'Lord Gyre,' said Miss Trumble thoughtfully. 'How odd that he should leave the Season right in the middle to come here.'

'He is a strange gentleman,' said Belinda. 'Perhaps the Season bores him.'

'Or perhaps he means to renew his acquaintance with the charms of Mrs. Ingram.'

'I do not know this Mrs. Ingram. Who is she?'

'A very dashing widow. I believe it was rumored that she was having an affair with Gyre about three years ago.'

'And so he has perhaps taken the opportunity of this house party to court her favours again?'

'Perhaps,' said Miss Trumble. 'Rumour always had it that it was Gyre who ended the liaison and not Mrs. Ingram.'

'I wish the whole sorry business was over with,' said Belinda.

Miss Trumble opened her mouth to say that surely the most sensible thing would be to persuade Lady Beverley to take her leave, but decided against it. Perhaps the dashing Mrs. Ingram was just the necessary ingredient to spark Belinda's interest in Lord Gyre.

Instead she talked comfortably about Brookfield House and how the hens were laying well because Barry sang to them. He swore the music of his voice increased the egg supply, although Miss Trumble said he sounded more like a corncrake than a nightingale.

And all the while Belinda wondered why Miss Trumble did not lecture her on the folly of wanting to marry St. Clair. Perhaps Miss Trumble did not care for her as much as she did for the others!

When the dressing-bell sounded, Miss Trumble rose and took her leave, promising to call again.

Betty, the maid from Brookfield House who now acted full-time as lady's-maid, came in to help Belinda to dress and arrange her hair.

With a feeling of nervousness, Belinda made her way to the drawing-room an hour later.

Her eyes went first to Mrs. Ingram. Belinda had never met her before but knew immediately who she was. She was the most striking lady in the room. She had flaming-red hair, as red as Lizzie's, but her eyes were bright blue. She had a voluptuous figure in a gold tissue gown which had been damped to make it cling even more closely to her body. She was talking to Lord Gyre, who seemed at ease in her company. Three girls stood together in front of the fireplace: the Hartley twins, Margaret and Polly, plump and dainty little brunettes, all rolling eyes, lisps and giggles; beside them stood Jane Chalmers, expensively gowned in the finest muslin and with her fine fair hair bound with a gold fillet. She had large grey eyes with fair lashes which surveyed the room with haughty contempt. Her mother was sitting on a sofa, also armoured in grand haughtiness. Mrs. Chalmers was bedecked with so many jewels pinned all over a black velvet gown that she looked rather like a town at night seen from the sea. Mr. and Mrs. Hartley, a small, plump couple, were chatting to Mirabel Dauncey and Lord St. Clair. Gurney Burke was entertaining Lady Beverley and Lizzie.

And then, just as Lord St. Clair was crossing the room to greet Belinda, the double doors were flung open and Jiggs intoned, 'The Honourable Peregrine Vane.'

Saint Clair had white-leaded his face. Cracks of sour disapproval began to run across his white lead mask as he surveyed his cousin.

'What brings you?' he asked.

'Uncle sent me down to see things were running smoothly.'

'They are, so you can turn around and go away.'

Perry threw Belinda a comically rueful look and she found herself smiling. 'Can't do that. I have your father's orders and you know he always expects them to be carried out.'

Saint Clair did not have the energy to be irritated for long. He gave a little shrug. 'Miss

Belinda, may I introduce my cousin, Mr. Vane. Perry, Miss Belinda Beverley.'

'Delighted to make your acquaintance,' said Perry. He was taken aback by Belinda's beauty. It was not just her beauty that was dangerous, he decided, but her almost sensual air of femininity, of vulnerability. Shrewd Perry saw immediately what even Belinda's sisters had failed to observe: that Belinda Beverley was not made of iron, and that at the back of her large eyes was a certain something that told him that far from being triumphant at being back at Mannerling again, Miss Belinda was heartily wishing herself somewhere else— anywhere else.

Across the room, Jane Chalmers's cool grey eyes studied Belinda as well. She had quite decided to make a play for St. Clair. Jane did not regard the dashing Mrs. Ingram as competition. She considered the widow little better than a member of the demi-monde and definitely not marriageable goods. Jane already coveted Mannerling. Earlier that day, the housekeeper had taken her on a tour of the place. She had marvelled at the beauty of the painted ceilings, at the fine plaster cornices, at the elegance of the double staircase rising out of the great hall. Through each long window lay a cool green vista of woods and gardens. She felt in an odd way that she had come home, that she could never, ever live in any other place again.

Although she admitted that Belinda was beautiful, she, too, had heard the girl was badly dowered and therefore did not anticipate much competition. Lizzie, covertly watching everything, saw Jane's assessing look, and her heart sank. It had all seemed so simple on the journey down to Mannerling. Now, as she saw it, Belinda was surrounded by rivals.

Dinner was announced. They entered in order of precedence, which meant that Lord St. Clair, as host, led Lady Beverley in, followed by Lord Gyre with Mrs. Chalmers on his arm. Belinda was near the rear, with Gurney Burke, and at the very end came Mrs. Ingram with Lizzie.

Lizzie was prepared to dislike what she privately damned as 'this fallen woman,' but Mrs. Ingram gave her a friendly smile and said, 'I see we both have red hair.'

'Such a social disadvantage,' mourned Lizzie. 'Red hair is so unfashionable.'

'Nonsense. It makes us both stand out in a crowd. Together we make everyone else look colourless.'

Lizzie found herself smiling back. 'See,' said Mrs. Ingram gaily, 'they have placed us both together at the end of the table, but we do not mind, do we? For we can have a comfortable coze.'

Feeling that she should neither be grateful for nor encourage such company, Lizzie gradually found she was enjoying herself. She did at first start to enthuse about the glories of Mannerling and about the wretched plight of the Beverleys when they had lost their home, but all Mrs. Ingram did was give her an infectious laugh and say teasingly, 'Now, my dear, it is a very grand and elegant place, but it is gone unless Saint Clair pops the question, and surely your sister is worth better than Saint Clair.'

'What is up with him?'

'He is an amiable fool, and although your sister is now playing the part of amiable fool as well, and to perfection, too, she will surely tire of the act.'

'But Lord Saint Clair would perhaps make an amiable husband?'

'I would not depend on that. Even fops, or should I say especially fops, have a nasty habit of becoming quite tyrannical when they are married. Have you considered that Saint Clair perhaps regards your sister in the light of a new waistcoat—something for the other bucks and beaux to stare at and envy? So what happens when she loses her looks? She will be tied to a boring chatterbox and he will be sulky and be-rate her for losing her face and figure, never stopping to consider that producing a child a year is apt to do just that.'

Lizzie gave a little shiver. She could feel all the old Mannerling obsession engulfing her.

'Are you cold?' she realized her new friend was asking her.

72

'No, it is just . . . Do you not feel this house has a presence?'

'No, although I have heard it is haunted. But despite my Scottish ancestry, I am not fey. The ghosts do not walk for me. Let us not talk about this boring old house. Tell me about your schooling. It is reported that you have a formidable governess.'

So Lizzie talked happily about Miss Trumble while Belinda flicked anxious little glances down the table, thinking her innocent little sister was being too familiar with a harpy.

At last Lady Beverley, who had assumed the role of hostess, rose to lead the ladies back to the drawing-room and leave the gentlemen to their wine.

The Hartley twins and Jane began to talk of balls and parties. Mrs. Chalmers and Mrs. Hartley studiously ignored Belinda, Lizzie, and Mrs. Ingram. Belinda at last joined Lizzie and Mrs. Ingram with a view to prizing her sister away from such contaminating company, but soon found herself falling victim to Mrs. Ingram's undoubted charm.

Belinda began to relax and entered into a lively discussion on whether the emancipation of the Jews would ever become a fact. She was aware that it was possibly dangerous to drop her silly act in front of this clever woman, but she felt she needed a rest from it before the gentlemen joined them.

When the gentlemen finally did, Jane was

urged by her mother to play the pianoforte. 'Lord Saint Clair will turn the pages of the music for you,' said her mother in the sort of commanding tone of voice which brooked no argument. As Lord St. Clair reluctantly drifted over to the piano, Mrs. Ingram rose and took Gurney Burke's arm and began to talk to him while Jane found her music, and Lady Beverley abruptly summoned Lizzie and Belinda to her side, angry that they should be so friendly with Mrs. Ingram. Lizzie went to join her, but Lord Gyre sank down on the sofa next to Belinda, and said, 'Talk to me. That is if you can talk sensibly. Never have I seen a young lady simper so dreadfully as you did at dinner.'

Belinda felt she ought to be insulted but found herself feeling amused instead. 'It was indeed a marathon performance,' she said. 'I thought I quite outdid myself.'

'Are you not worried that the fair and moneyed Miss Chalmers might not snatch Toby Saint Clair from under your nose?'

'I thought perhaps you yourself, my lord, were the target of her ambitions.'

'No, I fear Saint Clair is her quarry. Then you have another enemy.'

She looked at him questioningly.

'Mr. Vane.'

'I have done nothing to offend him!'

'I am unfashionable, you see, Miss Belinda.'

'And what has that to do with Mr. Vane's dislike of me, my lord?'

'You see,' said the marquess, stretching a pair of excellent legs in clocked silk stockings out in front of him, 'I listen to servants' gossip. Perry, Mr. Vane, was resident here before Saint Clair's arrival, and Mr. Vane was very much master of all he surveyed. I think he wants Mannerling for himself, and in order to get it he must make sure Saint Clair displeases his father. Now should Saint Clair succeed in announcing his betrothal, his father would be in alt, because the old earl wants grandchildren. Should something go wrong, should Saint Clair, for example, be shamed, then perhaps Mr. Vane's ambitions would be realized—that is, that the earl would disinherit his son and make Vane his heir.'

Belinda looked at him wide-eyed, but fell silent as Jane began to play. It was a long, boring piece which sounded like a series of Czerny piano exercises, which in fact it was, Jane having not progressed very far in her piano studies.

Belinda sat very still, suddenly acutely conscious of the tall strong figure next to her on the sofa. His thick black hair was swept back in two heavy wings from his handsome face and proud nose. She stole a sideways look at him, found him looking at her and blushed, not a delicate maidenly blush but fiery red. Her breath came quickly and she wished the music would end so that she could escape from his disturbing presence. Lord Gyre admired the

75

quick rise and fall of Belinda's excellent bosom and mentally chastised himself. He was not going to fall in love at this late age with a scheming minx who was proving to be a better actress than Mrs. Jordan.

At last Jane hit a final noisy chord. It was Lord Gyre who moved away to join Mrs. Ingram, and Gurney Burke and Lord St. Clair—moving quickly, for him—who crossed the room and took Gyre's place.

'Curst boring music, if you ask me, Miss Belinda.'

'Miss Chalmers plays with great verve, I think,' commented Belinda.

'If you say so. Don't know anything about music. I say, Miss Belinda, I heard some terrifying news about you.'

'You alarm me, my lord. What can it be?'

'That you are a bluestocking.'

Belinda dimpled prettily at him. 'Oh, no, my lord, my stockings are pink.' And she raised the hem of her gown an inch.

'I say,' said St. Clair, goggling at her. 'You're a bit of a goer.'

'Now, my lord.' Belinda gave him a playful rap with her fan. 'It is your attractions that make me overbold.'

Mirabel saw the couple on the sofa, saw the way his friend was goggling at Belinda and said hurriedly, 'What about cards? Silver loo? Piquet?'

Lady Beverley rang the bell and ordered the

card-tables to be brought in. Saint Clair, who was a dedicated gambler, promptly forgot about Belinda—which had been Mirabel's intention.

Perry played his usual cautious game while his mind worked busily. His sharp brain had picked out a possible ally in Mirabel; he suspected that Mirabel did not want his friend to marry Belinda Beverley, but would not be averse to the idea of St. Clair's marrying Jane Chalmers.

There must be some way, so ran his mind, of creating a disgrace at Mannerling, something so bad it would travel all the way to London and reach the ears of the earl. But he would wait and watch. He had hoped a scandal could be created through Mrs. Ingram, whose undoubted charms should have distracted his cousin. But it was being borne in on him, and not for the first time, that St. Clair was not overmuch interested in romance with the ladies. He frequented Cyprian balls, those elegant events held by the highest class of prostitute, but more because they were also frequented by such luminaries as Lord Byron rather than to partake in any of the sex which was so freely on offer.

Belinda, playing silver loo with the Hartley twins and Mrs. Ingram, let her mind wander from the game. If only Miss Trumble were here to give her a cool assessment of her chances. She suspected an enemy in Mirabel and felt she must move fast to secure a proposal from St. Clair. But this was only the first day of the house party. What easy company this Mrs. Ingram was. No wonder Gyre had ... had ... but Belinda's knowledge of sexual affairs was very limited and she could not envisage what a man did with a woman beyond kissing.

*   *   *

At last the party broke up and all went to bed, apart from St. Clair and Mirabel, who sat up drinking, with Mirabel trying to persuade his friend to propose to Jane Chalmers.

'Why?' was all St. Clair would say petulantly. 'People don't stare when the Chalmers chit goes by.'

'Belinda Beverley is only interested in you because of her ambitions to live here again,' sneered Mirabel.

Saint Clair leaned back in his chair, a drunken smile on his lips as he remembered that glimpse of pink stocking. 'Thash where you're wrong, old boy,' he drawled. 'Thash where you're wrong!'

CHAPTER THREE

'There's been an accident!' they said,
'Your servant's cut in half; he's dead!'
'Indeed!' said Mr. Jones, 'and please
Send me the half that's got my keys.'
                    —HARRY GRAHAM

Mrs. Ingram could not sleep because she was suddenly very hungry. She had eaten very little at dinner because that was the fashion. Ladies were supposed to pick at their food. It was two in the morning. Always considerate of servants, she decided not to ring the bell, but to make her way down to the kitchens and forage for something. She climbed down from the high old bed and pulled on a wrapper. She lit a bed candle and by the light of its wavering flame made her way out into the long corridor which led to the central staircase. As she walked carefully down to the first landing, holding on to the banister as she went and holding her candle high, eerie shadows flew away from her and up the walls.

And then, just as she reached the first landing, she became aware that the air was suddenly full of jingling, tinkling sounds like elfin laughter. She froze. Then she realized the sound was coming from the chandelier which hung over the great hall. Some lazy servant must have left a door or window open. But as she stood looking at the chandelier, which was at eye-level with the landing, she saw with fear that it was revolving a half turn one way, and then a half turn the other. She held her candle out. The steel cords which had been secured to the chandelier the day before had snapped. And as the crystals tinkled, she became aware of a feeling of brooding menace which seemed to emanate from the very walls. Dropping her candle, she scrambled back up the staircase, fled to her room, plunged into bed and pulled the covers tightly over her head.

Her maid awoke her in the morning and drew back the curtains to reveal a perfect sunny day.

Struggling up against the pillows, Mrs. Ingram remembered her terror of the night before. It all seemed so ridiculous now.

She said to her maid, 'Agnes, do run downstairs and find me something to eat. I tried to go down to the kitchens during the night and was frightened back upstairs by that wretched chandelier ... What is the matter?' For Agnes had let out a little scream.

'Oh, madam, they do say the house is haunted and that one of the previous owners, Mr. Judd, did hang himself from that very chandelier, and that during the night those steel cords did snap clean through.'

'Fiddle. Probably not secured properly.'

'Snapped clean through,' repeated Agnes firmly. 'We should leave, madam, before one of those ghosts catches us.'

'Ghosts? More than one?'

'Oh, yes. The servants do say that sometimes they see a drowned face in the lake, the face of a Mr. Cater, a sugar planter who was courting Rachel Beverley.'

'I refuse to believe in ghosts. What have they planned for us today?'

'You are to be ready by eleven o'clock. Lord St. Clair's organizing a boating party on the lake.'

'What an early hour to go rowing. Very well, fetch me some food to sustain me.'

*   *   *

At that moment, the Honourable Peregrine Vane was making his way to the lake with a thin saw hidden inside one of his boots. He resented the way St. Clair had ordered him like a servant to make sure there were enough boats for the whole party. He had been about to protest, but then he had hit on a wonderful plan. Saint Clair would no doubt take Belinda Beverley in the best boat. He got into the newest rowing-boat, which was tied up at the small wooden jetty, untied the painter, and rowed to a low grassy bank on the farther shore. There he pulled the boat clear of the water and got to work. He sawed a neat square hole in the bottom of the boat and then glued a piece of card over it. The card would become waterlogged and give way—he hoped—when St. Clair was in the

81

middle of the lake. Such a man-milliner as St. Clair would surely not be able to swim. Ladies did not swim, so Belinda Beverley would need to be rescued as well. He, Perry, would make sure news of the incident got back to the earl. No one would drown; there would be too many people present to help. But it would be a good start to the campaign he had in mind to disgrace St. Clair.

*   *   *

As they walked towards the lake later that morning, Lizzie found herself once more accompanied by Mrs. Ingram. 'I heard you suffered a fright during the night,' began Lizzie.

'That maid of mine is a terrible gossip,' said Mrs. Ingram. 'Ghosts, indeed!'

'But you were frightened?'

'My nerves were playing me tricks. The chandelier was revolving and tinkling and the steel cords had snapped. No headless ghosts, no rattling of chains. I fled to my room like the silly woman I am.'

'Perhaps Mannerling does not like you,' said Lizzie in a low voice.

'Mannerling does not . . .! My dear child, it is only a house. Houses do not have *feelings.*'

'This one does,' said Lizzie earnestly. 'I think it likes me.'

'Tish, child, what sort of nonsense is this?'

Lizzie averted her face. Mrs. Ingram remembered uneasily that feeling of almost tangible menace which had seemed to emanate from the walls.

'But why should it dislike me?' she asked in a light voice.

'Oh, Mannerling is like people,' said Lizzie, turning to look up at her companion. 'You know, you meet someone and take an instant dislike to them for no reason at all.'

'Enough of this,' said Mrs. Ingram, 'or I will begin to believe you and expect the house to start throwing slates at me. Only look at the poor gentlemen, such slaves of fashion. Here we are on this nice sunny day in our muslins and there they go in morning coats, starched cravats, and boots.'

'You are a friend of Lord Gyre, are you not?' asked Lizzie.

'Yes, and that is all I am, my pert miss with the green eyes. Ah, here we are.'

She stepped forward as Lord St. Clair was about to usher Belinda into the best rowing-boat. 'No, no,' said Mrs. Ingram gaily. 'Miss Belinda already knows all the delights of this place. You should row Miss Chalmers, and Gyre here can escort Miss Belinda.'

Saint Clair was too lazy to protest. The rest arranged themselves in the other boats, Mirabel rowing Lizzie and Mrs. Ingram.

'So here we are,' said the marquess. 'May I say you are looking divinely pretty, Miss

83

Belinda?'

'You may say so, my lord, if it pleases you. Whether I believe you or not is another matter.'

'There are times when I wish you would flirt with me as you do with Saint Clair.'

'You would know me to be false.'

'But I might enjoy the falsehood.'

'Why, my lord?'

'Because you enchant me, Belinda Beverley.'

'Now is you who are only flirting. Your eyes are mocking. Only look at Lord Saint Clair. He is rowing very strongly. I would not have thought him possessed of either the skill or the energy.'

Lord St. Clair was enjoying himself. Jane Chalmers was praising him fulsomely and he was thinking her a splendid sort of girl when she broke off a fluttering comment on his strength and let out a shriek.

'What's amiss?' he demanded, shipping the oars.

'My feet are wet,' she wailed. 'Water is coming into the boat.'

Saint Clair looked down. Her thin slippers had felt the water quicker than his booted feet. 'Get the bailer,' he was starting to say when the waterlogged card gave entirely and the boat sank like a stone—and so did Jane Chalmers.

Before he had become a dandy, St. Clair had hoped to become a member of the Corinthian set and so had learned to fence and swim and drive a four-in-hand. Their energy, their spitting and swearing had offended his delicate nerves, but had left him with the ability to swim like a fish. He surfaced, dived, grabbing hold of Jane's dress, hauled her to the surface and began to head for the bank, holding her tightly. Lord Gyre was there before him. Once he had seen that St. Clair could swim, he had rowed energetically for the bank. Jane had fortunately closed her mouth tightly when she sank and so she was soaking and shaken but not otherwise harmed, and retained enough of her wits to quickly see the romantic advantages of the situation. Thrusting aside her mother, who had appeared on the scene, Jane stumbled to her feet and threw herself into St. Clair's arms, crying, 'My hero! I owe you my life!'

Mirabel looked on fondly. So much for Belinda Beverley and her ambitions.

'I think Miss Chalmers should be taken directly to the house and put to bed,' said Lady Beverley crossly. She flashed an irritated glance at her daughter. Why couldn't it have been Belinda who had nearly been drowned?

After Jane was led away, Lord St. Clair sat down on the grass and took off one boot, emptied out the lake water, and then glared all around. 'Ah, there you are, Perry,' he said crossly, espying his cousin, who was trying to sidle away. 'You said you would see to things. Didn't you notice the boat was leaky?'

'I am not your servant,' retorted Perry

furiously. 'I only checked there were enough boats for the party.'

Lord Gyre turned to Belinda. 'How deep is the lake?'

'Where the boat sank? I am not sure. About fourteen feet of water, I think.'

'We should get two men to dive down with ropes and try to lift the boat up,' said Lord Gyre.

'Why?' demanded Perry.

'I just want to make sure no one had been tampering with it.'

'That's ridiculous,' expostulated Perry. 'The planks probably had sprung in the heat.'

'Nonetheless, I would like to make sure.'

'Then you organize it,' said Perry, and strode off towards the house.

'Why bother?' said St. Clair, standing up. 'I'm thirsty. Let's all go back and have some luncheon.'

Lord Gyre walked off in the direction of the stables and the rest of the party made their way back to the house.

'That was an interesting accident,' said Mrs. Ingram, falling into step beside Belinda. 'If it was an accident.'

'I think it must have been,' said Belinda. 'If anyone wanted to drown Saint Clair, they would hardly try to do so when so many people and servants were about.'

'The plan may have been to disgrace him.'

'Well, if that was the case, it sadly missed.

Saint Clair is the hero of the day.'

'I think Perry Vane might have been behind it some way. In fact, if you want to regain Mannerling, I would concentrate your attentions on Mr. Vane. He means to have the place, of that I am sure.'

Belinda moved rapidly away from her. Mrs. Ingram gave a rueful shrug. Now I have been much too impertinent, she thought.

Lizzie scampered after her sister. 'You almost ran away from Mrs. Ingram, Belinda. Did she say something to offend you?'

'She suggested I should concentrate on Perry Vane because he means to discredit Saint Clair and gain Mannerling for himself.'

'He must not succeed,' said Lizzie fiercely.

'Why?' demanded Belinda drily. 'I thought it did not matter whom I married as long as I got Mannerling.'

'But I cannot like Mr. Vane. And we were agreed that Saint Clair would make an amiable husband. Did you hear that Mrs. Ingram was haunted during the night?'

'I heard she was frightened by the tinkling of the chandelier, nothing more. Mrs. Ingram has too vivid an imagination and sees ghostly happenings and Gothic plots everywhere she looks. And yet, if she had any sensitivity, she would take herself off.'

'Why?'

'Because she is Gyre's ex-mistress,' said Belinda crossly. 'You would think any woman of breeding and delicacy would find the situation distressful.'

'They seem the best of friends,' said Lizzie, 'which all goes to show that Gyre is not the man for you.'

'Stop talking fustian,' snapped Belinda. 'I have no interest in Gyre whatsoever.'

She walked faster and Lizzie scurried to keep up. 'You see,' panted Lizzie, 'I am afraid history will repeat itself and you will be like our elder sisters and throw up the chance of Mannerling for love.'

Belinda stopped and faced her. 'Our sisters decided not to marry highly unsuitable men and as a result are all happy.'

'I knew it! You are interested in Gyre.'

'Lizzie, you are making my poor head ache. If only we could talk to Miss Trumble. I feel the need of some sensible conversation.'

*   *   *

Later that day, Lord Gyre, followed by two grooms who claimed to be excellent swimmers and also by a farm labourer leading a sturdy horse, headed for the lake.

The idea was that the grooms were to dive down where the rowing-boat had sunk and attach ropes to it, which would then be fastened to the halter on the horse. Then the horse would be backed away from the lake and so pull the boat out.

The grooms stripped off, chattering cheerfully to each other and obviously treating it all as a bit of an adventure.

Lord Gyre waited patiently as each man with a rope in his hand dived into the lake, swam to where the boat had sunk, and dived again. It was only a few moments before both surfaced, gasping and spluttering and then swimming frantically for the shore. They scrambled out. 'What on earth are you about?' demanded the marquess wrathfully.

'There's a drowned man down there, m'lord,' gasped one. 'I was groom at stables when the previous owner was here. It was that Mr. Cater, the sugar planter, him what used to call. He . . . reached out his hands for me.'

'Dolts,' said the marquess savagely. 'Oh, I'll do it myself. Thank God the ropes are floating on the surface.'

He stripped off, tossing his clothes at his feet, strode to the water's edge and dived in.

As he managed to locate the boat by feel, he wondered furiously how those idiots had managed to see anything at all at the bottom. He attached one rope, surfaced, and swam back with it and threw it on the bank, where one white-faced groom fastened it to the horse's collar. The marquess then swam back and repeated the process with the other rope.

The farm horse was backed slowly up the bank and gradually, with the men helping, the boat was pulled to the shore and up the grassy bank. Naked, with water running down his body, the marquess bent down and examined the boat carefully. Then he stood up.

'Someone sawed a hole in the bottom of this boat. Something must have been put over the hole to cover it so that it would sink after a certain time.'

Lizzie and Belinda, who had gone out for a walk, had entered the folly. They looked down at the tableau by the lake—two naked grooms and an equally naked marquess. Lizzie let out a squeak and then covered her eyes with her hands. Belinda finally dragged her own eyes away and led Lizzie out of the folly and back towards the house.

'I did not know naked men looked like that,' said Lizzie at last.

'We have seen classical statues,' said Belinda in a bracing voice which belied the fact that she was quite shaken and that the statues she had seen had all worn decorous marble fig-leaves.

* * *

The marquess had urged the grooms not to talk nonsense about a drowned man in the lake, but then he became anxious that there might really be a body down there and informed the authorities. The house party gathered again at the lake as it was dragged by a team of men from the nearby market town of Hedgefield.

Somehow, the marquess was not surprised

90

when the search was finally over without anything being found. He wondered then whether to turn the authorities' attention to the rowing-boat but decided against it. Perry would only protest hotly that he had had nothing to do with it and the house party would be made miserable by scandal.

He found himself gravitating towards Belinda, a cool figure in the inevitable white muslin considered suitable for young girls.

'Did you expect to find a drowned man?' she asked.

'Not really,' he said with a smile. One of her black curls had come loose and was lying against the whiteness of her neck. He had a sudden impulse to wind that glossy curl around his fingers.

'Do you not plan to visit your home while you are here?' he asked.

Belinda gave a little sigh. 'I would like to call on my governess, Miss Trumble. She is an estimable lady.'

'Then perhaps you will allow me the honour of driving you there tomorrow.'

'Lizzie, too?' asked Belinda, ignoring a little snort of disapproval from Lizzie, who had heard this exchange.

'Of course. Shall we say eleven o'clock tomorrow morning?'

He noticed her hesitation and said gently, 'Today was unusual. Saint Clair does not rise until two in the afternoon. You will be back in plenty of time to resume the hunt.'

Belinda gave a reluctant laugh. 'I feel I should not let you talk to me on such terms.'

'I think you find it a relief to let down your guard and be honest.'

Gurney Burke watched Belinda and his friend with narrowed eyes. That Gyre, who had remained a bachelor so long, should fall for nothing better than a scheming adventuress called Belinda Beverley was too much. Gurney found himself joined by Mirabel, who languidly waved his quizzing-glass in the direction of Belinda and the marquess. 'It seems as if my friend, Saint Clair, is no longer a target.'

'Fustian,' said Gurney crossly. 'Gyre is a confirmed bachelor.'

'Doesn't look that way at the moment,' said Mirabel airily. 'But he has no chance. Belinda Beverley wants Mannerling and Saint Clair wants Belinda Beverley, and there's nothing can be done about it and I, for one, only want to see my friend happy,' with Jane Chalmers, he added silently.

Perry, too, observed the couple, but with satisfaction. The earl would be furious if the house party ended without St. Clair's becoming betrothed. But Jane Chalmers was a difficulty. If she turned out to be the chosen one, then the earl would be even more delighted. Jane Chalmers was a rich heiress. Perry discounted the Hartley twins. Saint Clair hadn't even seemed to notice their existence.

92

marry him and fled to escape arrest. Nothing was heard of him since. Perhaps he was drowned at sea.'

'So you believe there is a ghost ... that people see the drowned Mr. Cater in the lake?'

'I assure you, my lord,' said Miss Trumble, 'that before I ever visited Mannerling, I did not believe in anything supernatural at all.'

'I confess I begin to take a dislike to the place,' said Lord Gyre. 'How pleasant it is here! I declare I find myself reluctant to return.'

Miss Trumble smiled. 'You may stay as long as you like.'

'Ah, my revered lady, I must point out that Miss Belinda is anxious to return to the hunt.'

Belinda coloured as Lizzie threw her a fulminating glance and Miss Trumble a reproving one.

'Belinda always did have a puckish sense of humour,' said Miss Trumble quickly. 'You must not take her too seriously, my lord.'

'I assure you, Miss Trumble, I do not take her seriously at all.'

The minute the words were out of his mouth, he regretted them. This grand governess made him feel as if he had been childish and rude. And yet, he had become used to being chased and courted and fêted. The fact that Belinda Beverley obviously did not find him attractive in the least rankled in an increasingly unpleasant way.

He recovered quickly and said blandly, 'That was said in the wrong way. I find the fascination Mannerling appears to hold for everyone extremely irritating. It causes a false air of menace to permeate the rooms of the place and leads to the servants' tattling about ghosts.'

'It is an odd place,' said Miss Trumble while her brain worked furiously. Gyre had referred lightly to Belinda's 'hunt', which probably meant that Belinda had actually discussed her ambitions to secure St. Clair with this highly eligible man. How on earth could Belinda or any other woman look at St. Clair with a prize like Gyre around! She longed for a private word with Belinda but could not think how to engineer it. Then she saw Barry coming around the corner of the house and hailed him. As Barry came up to them, Miss Trumble said, 'We are most proud of our vegetable garden, my lord. Would you care to see it?'

The marquess looked surprised, but said politely, 'Yes, I would.'

Miss Trumble waved one thin, elegant hand. 'Barry, do conduct my lord to the vegetable garden. Belinda, there is something I want to show you.'

Belinda reluctantly followed Miss Trumble into the house. 'No, not you this time, Lizzie,' said Miss Trumble quietly as Lord Gyre disappeared with Barry.

Lizzie pouted but returned obediently to the table in the garden.

Miss Trumble led the way into the parlour and turned to face Belinda. 'Now, young miss,' she began sternly, 'what are you about, to confide your ambitions so freely to Lord Gyre?'

'I did not . . .' began Belinda, and then she shrugged. 'It seemed better to tell the truth,' she confessed. 'Everyone learns sooner or later about the Beverleys' ambitions.'

Miss Trumble forgot all her good resolutions to let Belinda make her own mistakes and lead her own life. 'Are your wits wandering?' she demanded. 'Here is a handsome, rich, and eligible man. I had hopes . . .' She bit her lip. 'Belinda, I am fond of you. I am fond of you all. I did not mean to criticize or interfere. But it infuriates me that you are prepared to ally yourself to a useless fop for the rest of your life and, yes, to bear his stupid children when you might have had a man like Gyre.'

Belinda looked at her haughtily. 'I am persuaded Mama has the right of it and you forget your position in our household. You praise Gyre, yet what do you know of him? He is too old for me, and not only that, he parades his mistress Mrs. Ingram, at Mannerling. This Mrs. Ingram is of the house party.'

'I have heard nothing but good of Mrs. Ingram,' said Miss Trumble, suddenly heartily weary of the Beverleys and all their machinations.

'And what can you possibly have heard?'

demanded Belinda. 'You are not exactly in society.'

'I hear a great deal more than you could possibly imagine, miss. Gyre is in his early thirties and a man like that could not be expected to live like a monk. Oh, forget what I said. Do what you wish.'

Belinda felt herself crumple. She had hoped that a lecture from Miss Trumble on the folly of chasing St. Clair would have strengthened her resolve to do just that, but here, in her home and away from Mannerling, she could feel her resolve ebbing away.

'We must not quarrel, Miss Trumble,' said Belinda. 'Come, smile at me. We have been friends for so long.'

'A friend who is all too often reminded of her place.'

'I was annoyed. You must not stand between me and Mannerling.'

'I think Mannerling does what it wants,' said Miss Trumble, but in such a low voice that Belinda could not make out what it was she had said.

Lizzie looked anxiously at her sister as she and Miss Trumble walked back towards the table in the garden. Lord Gyre came back at the same time, remarking, 'What a splendid garden. You're lucky to have found Barry.'

'We are indeed,' agreed Miss Trumble. 'I do not know what we would do without him.'

'He is a servant,' snapped Lizzie, 'and one

can always replace servants.' She then quailed under an icy look from Miss Trumble and flushed as red as her hair. Belinda quickly began to talk about the fine weather. Lizzie felt miserable. She adored Barry and yet felt he was in league with Miss Trumble in trying to stop Belinda's marrying St. Clair. And Belinda must marry St. Clair. All the humiliations and frights her elder sisters had undergone were forgotten along with her own good resolutions never to let the house get a grip on her again. So Lizzie sat silently, praying to God to return the Beverleys to Mannerling.

At last, to Lizzie's relief, Belinda said they must leave. 'A charming home and a charming governess,' said Lord Gyre as they drove off. 'Do you not miss your home?'

'We miss Mannerling very much,' said Lizzie eagerly.

Belinda laughed. 'He means Brookfield House. It is not such fun as it was, my lord, since our sisters have left. But, yes, I have grown accustomed to the place.'

The weather was glorious; warm sunshine bathed the fields in a golden glow. A field of flax looked like a fallen piece of sky, and trees heavy with leaves arched over the road.

Belinda felt strangely happy. She had the treacherous thought that it would be infinitely preferable if she could amble on through the beautiful countryside with this handsome companion and no longer gear herself up to entrap such a man as St. Clair. But had she had any romantical thoughts about Lord Gyre—and she had not, she told herself firmly—she would have put paid to them by her confidences about her unmaidenly ambitions.

For his part, Lord Gyre considered it was as well the ferocious little Lizzie was acting as chaperone. He glanced sideways at Belinda's pink lips and wondered what it would be like to kiss them, wondered if he could rouse passion in her. Ladies were not supposed to feel passion, only women did, and yet, Belinda was unusual. He was intensely aware of the light scent she wore and the slim yet voluptuous body under the thin muslin gown. Had he had serious intentions towards Belinda Beverley—and he had not!—then the very presence of his ex-mistress would have put paid to them. So while Lizzie fretted privately that they were making their way too slowly, Belinda and Lord Gyre sat wrapped in their thoughts.

*   *   *

Mrs. Ingram had been found in that masculine sanctum, the billiard-room, by Lord St. Clair. Billiards was an old indoor game which had fallen into abeyance rather like the game of trap and ball, although the latter was still flourishing in America under the name of baseball. The *Morning Post* had recently stated: 'Billiards are becoming very fashionable; it is an amusement of a gentlemanly cast—giving at once activity to the limbs and grace to the person.'

There was even an undisputed billiards champion, a Mr. Andrews, who had reached such a degree of perfection that no one in Europe could rival him. He lived on nothing but tea and toast and was obsessed with the game. He could have made his fortune but was an inveterate gambler. One night, he won ten thousand pounds from a colonel who arranged to meet him the next day to go with him to the City and transfer stock to him for the amount owing. Being in a hackney coach, they tossed up for who should pay for it. Andrews lost the first toss and would not give up. By the time the pair reached the City, he had lost all, and when the coachman stopped to let them get down, he was ordered to get up again and drive them back, as they had no occasion to get out. He retired to Kent to live on a small annuity which was so tied up that he could not gamble it away and found contentment at last, living on a pittance.

'What are you doing here?' demanded St. Clair. Mrs. Ingram smiled, took a cue and bent over the table, exposing a generous bosom. 'Looking for a game,' she said.

'Ladies don't play,' sneered St. Clair.

'This one does. I tell you what, I'll lay you a wager.'

'What wager?'

'If you lose, you kiss me. If you win, you get five hundred pounds.'

'You're mad!'

Mrs. Ingram gave an almost boyish grin. 'Confident, that is all. Do we play, or are you frightened a mere woman will beat you?'

'Not I!' said St. Clair. 'If you have five hundred pounds to throw away, that is your business.'

Lord St. Clair prided himself with his expertise at billiards. He was mortified when Mrs. Ingram beat him easily. 'It's not fair!' he cried petulantly. 'It is because I am playing with a lady. I let you win!'

She gave him a slow seductive smile. 'You must want to kiss me very much.'

He did not, but a bet was a bet. He approached her and pursed up his lips and closed his eyes.

She took his weak face between her hands and kissed him very gently on the lips. He found to his surprise that the experience was comforting. She released him and said huskily, 'I fear you have won my heart.'

Saint Clair goggled at her. Then he grinned, what he thought a wicked, doggish sort of grin. 'Teach you to play with fire, lady.'

'Oh, yes.' Mrs. Ingram lowered her eyelashes. He noticed for the first time that they were long and thick and black. He found himself attracted to a lady for the first time. But somewhere in his not-too-agile brain alarm bells were beginning to sound. His father would certainly not approve of Gyre's cast-off, and he, St. Clair, had not been in the way of keeping a mistress and shrank from the idea.

'M'father wouldn't like it,' he blurted out and fled from the billiard-room.

Mrs. Ingram sat down on the window-seat. She was unfazed by St. Clair's remark. But although she had hitherto meant to distract St. Clair from Belinda, now she began to wonder whether she should really try to get St. Clair to marry *her*. That would involve somehow meeting the earl and charming the old boy. She summed up the pros and cons. She was of good ton despite her doubtful reputation and was rich, but she was older than St. Clair. Still, it might be amusing to try. And she thought Gyre and the fair Belinda were very well suited.

Then there was the challenge of Mannerling. Like Miss Trumble, she had never considered herself superstitious, and yet she felt somehow the house was against her. If she married St. Clair, she could persuade him to sell. All this plotting and planning cheered her. She did not regard Jane Chalmers or the giggling, simpering twins as any competition whatsoever. Belinda, she felt sure, did not in her heart of hearts want to marry St. Clair, and yet there was the peculiar hold this house had on the Beverleys.

That evening an impromptu dance was held. Musicians had been summoned from

Hedgefield. Gurney and Mirabel danced with the twins, St. Clair with Belinda, and Lord Gyre took Lizzie onto the floor. Mrs. Ingram sat and fanned herself and watched and waited, noticing with amusement the way St. Clair's eyes kept straying in her direction. Perry noticed those glances too and his eyes narrowed with speculation. He wondered whether he might offer Mrs. Ingram a bribe to use her wiles on St. Clair and then decided against it. Everyone knew Mrs. Ingram was rich.

So they danced on, Belinda uncomfortably aware of the marquess, he of her, and St. Clair looking, always looking, to where Mrs. Ingram sat fanning herself.

Lord Gyre called for a waltz and asked Belinda to dance, and Lord St. Clair persuaded himself it would be only polite to talk to Mrs. Ingram.

'Such a hot evening,' said Mrs. Ingram languidly. 'I have been looking out at the rose garden. I think I will leave you to your dancing and take a turn in the evening air.'

'I would accompany you, dear lady,' said Lord St. Clair gallantly, 'but I cannot leave my guests.'

'Why not?' She tickled his nose with the feathered end of her fan.

'S'pose I could,' he said, feeling that odd quickening of the senses.

'There is no need to make a fuss. We could

just slip away for a little.' Her large eyes flirted at him over the fan.

He had that heady feeling of being a rip, a slayer of ladies' hearts. 'I shall dance you to the door,' he whispered.

No one but the ever-watchful Perry saw them go. Belinda, with Lord Gyre's hand at her waist, was feeling quite dizzy with a whole series of new emotions. Lord Gyre noticed the heightened colour on her cheeks and decided it would be only fair to the girl to try to make her fall in love with him. She was too good for such as St. Clair.

Somehow, in the peace of the rose garden, Lord St. Clair found himself telling Mrs. Ingram all his woes, about being pressured into marriage, about never being able to please his father.

How warm and sweet the comforting darkness of the rose garden was, and how sympathetic was Mrs. Ingram. No one had ever listened to him like this before. As a crescent moon rose in the dark-blue sky above and a heady scent of roses surrounded them, he droned on about the beatings he had had from his tutor and his father, how he just wanted an easy life roistering around with his friends.

'You will become tired of running around sooner or later,' said Mrs. Ingram at last. 'You will want a son. A fine young man like you should have someone in his own image.'

'But marriage and all that . . .' Lord St. Clair

waved a hand as if to encompass all the trials of wedding and wooing.

'It might be easier than you think,' cooed Mrs. Ingram. 'You have great sensibility and that makes you worry too much. A companionable lady who understood you would be just the thing.'

Perry, who had noticed the couple were missing and had tracked them down to the rose garden, stood listening behind a bush. He rubbed his hands gleefully. Here was news at last for the earl. Mannerling was as good as his!

CHAPTER FOUR

A noble Lord, lately high in office, and who manifests a strong inclination to be reinstated in his political power, lost at the Union, a night or two back, 4,000 guineas before twelve o'clock; but continuing to play, his luck took a turn, and he rose a winner of a thousand before five the next morning.

—*MORNING HERALD, June 16, 1804*

The following day, Lord Gyre rose early and, wrapped in a banan, made his way to the morning-room. He planned to spend a peaceful hour before anyone else was awake reading the newspapers. But when he pushed open the door of the morning room, he saw Belinda seated at the table, her head bent over a newspaper. She was wearing an old blue cotton gown and her hair had not been put up. Shining, black and curly, it lay on her shoulders.

He would have retreated, but she looked up and saw him, and said, 'Good morning, my lord.' Her eyes were wide and friendly. Once again he experienced that sharp feeling of pique that this beauty should be so apparently unaware of him as a man.

He sat down opposite her. 'Anything of interest?'

She smiled. 'Only things that enrage me.'

'Such as?'

'Wife-selling.'

'Ah. Well, that does not go on in our rarefied stratum of society.'

'Just listen to this: "A man named John Gorsthorpe exposed his wife for sale in the market at Hull; but owing to the crowd which such an extraordinary occurrence had gathered together, he was obliged to defer the sale, and take her away. About four o'clock, however, he again brought her out and she was sold for twenty guineas, and delivered, in a halter, to a person named Houseman, who had lodged with them for four or five years." Is that not dreadful?'

The marquess's eyes mocked her. 'Twenty guineas is a fair sum. The lodger must have wanted her badly.'

'Then if that does not shock your cynical soul, do but listen to this! "One of those disgraceful scenes, which have, of late, become too common, took place on Friday se'nnight at Knaresborough. Owing to some jealousy, or other family difference, a man brought his wife in a halter and sold her at the market cross for sixpence and a quid of tobacco!" '

Belinda rustled the paper furiously. 'Women are not gaining any more respect or equality in this modern world. We are retreating into the Dark Ages.'

'Not really. Such sales have been going on among the lower orders since time immemorial.'

'And since times immemorial,' flashed Belinda, 'nothing has been done by the authorities to stop this dreadful trade. So it is not only the lower orders who have not progressed but the higher orders, too.'

'There are worse ills abroad in the world—murder, rape, and pillage.'

'Perhaps,' she said tartly, 'because it is a world run by men!'

'You are indeed a bluestocking, Miss Belinda.'

'Not I. If I were a bluestocking I might have more dignity and sense than to try to sell myself for this wretched house.'

Then she looked at him aghast, hardly able to believe what she had just said. Outside, a cloud crossed the sun, plunging the morning-room into darkness, and a sudden wind blew around the house like a great sigh.

A faint tinkling sound reached their ears. The chandelier.

The Beverleys were not Roman Catholics, and yet Belinda crossed herself. 'Forgive me, my lord,' she said, and Lord Gyre wondered whether it had been an apology to himself or to God.

Sunlight streamed into the room again. 'I sometimes chafe at the restrictions put upon women,' Belinda went on. 'The terrible tyranny of marriage and after that, a baby each year. Mostly, I am content to play the game, to wear pretty clothes and to flirt. But were I a man, I could fight in the wars and perhaps gain enough prize money to—' She broke off in confusion.

'You were about to say, "... gain enough prize money to buy Mannerling." You interest me, Miss Belinda, and not just because of your pretty face. You appear intelligent, except when it comes to Mannerling, and then all your good sense disappears. You think Saint Clair would be an easy man to live with because you know he detests the country and you imagine a marriage in name only. But he is under his father's thumb, and his father will want grandchildren as soon as possible. Then think of the days when you are both old and you have a fop without brains or character to take care of in your declining years.'

Belinda looked at him haughtily. 'There will be servants enough to take care of him.'

'Ah, but as you have brought to my attention, women have no say in anything. Once you are married to Saint Clair, you are his to do with exactly as he likes.'

She suddenly remembered how the marquess had looked naked, and the thought flashed into her mind that there could be, for her, perhaps, some man whose domination she would enjoy. Then she blushed painfully and deeply again.

'We have fallen into the way of talking too openly,' he said gently. 'Such is not usual between a man and a woman. You are very outspoken, and yet I confess I would not have you any other way.'

A piercing stab of happiness entered Belinda's heart at those words, and her face became almost translucent. He rose and leaned over her, and her heart hammered against her ribs.

Then the door of the morning-room opened and Lizzie came in. The marquess sat down suddenly and Belinda said crossly, 'What are you doing up and about this early, Lizzie?'

'Looking for you,' said Lizzie, her green eyes darting suspiciously from one to the other.

'Excuse me, ladies,' said the marquess. He bowed and left the room.

'What was going on?' demanded Lizzie. 'I thought he was going to kiss you!'

'Nonsense!' exclaimed Belinda. 'Lord Gyre was merely leaning forward to take up a newspaper.'

'I think you are going to be like the others,' said Lizzie, meaning their elder sisters. 'I think you are going to throw away a chance at getting Mannerling back.'

'Not I!' said Belinda with a lightness she did not feel. Had he been going to kiss her? What would that have been like?'

Gurney Burke opened the door of the morning-room a little, saw the girls and was about to retreat when Lizzie's next words froze him.

'Of course,' Lizzie said eagerly, 'Gyre is very rich indeed. There is always the possibility that you could get him to buy Mannerling for you as a wedding gift.'

And Belinda, who had been badly shaken by the tumult of feelings caused in her breast by Lord Gyre and was anxious to return to her old image of being strong and confident, said with a laugh, 'Perhaps I might consider Gyre if my wiles fail to work on Saint Clair. It is always as well to have one in reserve, don't you think?'

Lizzie gave a trill of laughter. 'Now that is more like the dear sister I know.'

Gurney retreated, his face dark with anger.

'Was that someone at the door?' Belinda asked sharply. 'And it is open a little way. I am sure Lord Gyre closed it behind him.'

Lizzie darted to the door, opened it wide and looked outside. 'There is no one there at all,' she said.

Lord Gyre was adjusting his cravat when Gurney strolled into his room. 'Morning, Gurney,' said the marquess. 'You look like the devil.'

'I have just overheard a most interesting conversation,' said Gurney. He repeated almost what he had overheard but made it seem much worse by adding the embellishment that Belinda had said, 'I can have Gyre any time I want.'

The marquess did not feel angry. He only felt a great weariness of spirit. Since he had come of age, he had been ruthlessly pursued. Débutantes had pretended to faint in his arms, matchmaking mamas and their eager daughters had even pursued him to his home in the country, and he had been naïve enough to think that Belinda was beginning to be attracted to him, that she had brains and character.

'I am sorry to disillusion you,' said Gurney, beginning to feel guilty that he had lied, if only a little. 'There are ladies a-plenty who would love you for yourself alone.'

'Take away my title and my fortune and I doubt if any of them would give me a second glance,' said Lord Gyre. 'Shall we go for a gallop? And then we will perhaps decide to leave. This place wearies me. There is, however, someone in the neighborhood I think you should meet.'

'And who is that?'

'A Miss Trumble.'

'And who is Miss Trumble?'

'The Beverley girls' governess.'

'I do not think that is a good idea, nor do I wish to meet a governess who has no doubt instilled—or at best failed to curb—such unmaidenly ambitions in her charges.'

'I think you will find she has done everything she could to quench them. Trust me. She is not in the common way.'

*　　　*　　　*

Gurney uneasily felt, when they arrived at Brookfield House, that his friend was still besotted with Belinda, else why would he wish to visit this old creature who had answered the door herself, dressed in an old gown and a baize apron.

'I was working in the still-room, gentlemen,' said Miss Trumble, 'and you must forgive my dress. But come into the garden and the maid will bring us some refreshment. I have just made this morning a pitcher of lemonade.'

When they were seated in the garden under the cedar tree, Gurney noticed the governess had quickly changed into a very modish gown. 'And how are things at Mannerling?' asked Miss Trumble.

Startled, Gurney heard the marquess say

coldly, 'I regret to inform you that your charges are plotting and planning as usual.'

'You already knew they were plotting and planning,' said Miss Trumble, her eyes moving from Gurney's face to the marquess's and back again. Gurney shifted uneasily in his chair.

'I did not know quite how ruthless they could be,' said the marquess. 'My friend here heard a most unsettling conversation between Misses Belinda and Lizzie.'

'Overheard conversations that are not meant for one's ears can often be unsettling,' said Miss Trumble.

'I felt I had to warn my friend,' said Gurney hotly. 'It was my duty.'

'Pray enlighten me,' said Miss Trumble.

The marquess repeated what Gurney had overheard. Miss Trumble listened carefully until Belinda's supposed last sentence that she could have Gyre any time she wanted.

'Belinda is headstrong and wilful, I admit,' said Miss Trumble, looking steadily at Gurney, 'but she is not vain, despite her looks. Most of what you say you heard, Mr. Burke, has the ring of truth, but such as Belinda Beverley would never say that she could have the marquess here any time she wanted.'

Gurney flushed and his eyes darted about the garden. But, he thought quickly, if he admitted he had lied about that little bit, then Gyre would assume he had lied about the whole, and his friend had to be protected

116

against the machinations of the Beverleys. 'I repeated only what I had heard,' he said stiffly. 'I am not in the way of being taken for a liar.'

Miss Trumble gave him a kindly look which made him feel worse. So his mother had once looked on him when he was a small boy and he had sworn he had not stolen the local farmer's apples when his pockets had been bulging with them.

'In any case, I am tired of this visit,' said Lord Gyre, 'and mean to depart to London on the morrow.'

'I think it is time I returned there myself,' said Miss Trumble. 'How goes Lady Beverley?'

'I have not seen very much of her,' said the marquess. 'She is poorly but refuses the attentions of the physician.'

'I will wait here until the family decide to return to London and then I will depart. I have been neglecting my duties.'

The marquess looked at her curiously. 'Surely your duties are over. The ladies are old enough to do without the services of a governess.'

'Belinda is nineteen years and Lizzie, eighteen,' said Miss Trumble. 'But Lady Beverley is often ill and the girls need someone to guide them. Yes, I shall go back to London. I am only sorry you—or rather Mr. Burke here—overheard such a conversation. But as the Beverleys are not your concern, my lord, that should not trouble you overmuch.'

'You have the right of it,' he said bitterly. 'Belinda Beverley is nothing to me.'

But she was, thought Miss Trumble sadly, until your friend here interfered.

*   *   *

Belinda dressed that evening with more than her usual care. Although she had wandered through the rooms of the great house and out around the grounds, she had seen no sign of Lord Gyre. She found she could not think of St. Clair. All she could think of was the marquess, of his dark handsome face, his long strong legs, his firm yet sensitive mouth. As Betty pinned the last artificial silk rose among Belinda's glossy curls, Belinda's heartbeats quickened. She would soon see him again.

As she made her way a few minutes later along the corridor and down the stairs to the drawing-room, her elation began to ebb. She began to feel a dark, brooding disappointment that seemed to emanate from the very walls.

As she reached the first landing, there was a brilliant flash of lightning which set the crystals of the chandelier flickering with blue light. Then there was a loud crash of thunder.

Belinda bit back a cry of fright and headed for the drawing-room. A footman sprang to open the double doors.

Her mother was there reclining wanly on a sofa. The Hartley twins were clutching each

118

other and looking out of the window at the breaking storm. The lamps and candles had not yet been lit. The marquess, who was standing with Mrs. Ingram by the fireplace, looked across at her. Another flash of lightning lit his stern face, and then he turned to Mrs. Ingram and began to say something.

Belinda knew in that moment that she had been dismissed, that he had taken her in disgust. The Hartley twins, Margaret and Polly, and Jane Chalmers had never liked Belinda or Lizzie much, seeing Belinda in particular as just so much unwanted competition. Lord St. Clair only seemed to want to be in the orbit of Mrs. Ingram, and Gurney Burke was sending Belinda little glances of distaste, and so Belinda felt grubby and diminished. Only Mirabel talked to her pleasantly, his worried eyes going from her downcast face to St. Clair's happy one, St. Clair happy because Mrs. Ingram was paying more attention to him than she was to Lord Gyre.

Perry Vane looked out at the storm. The trees below the window were thrashing back and forth and throwing their branches up to the tumbling black sky. He had sent an express to the earl about his son's 'liaison' with Mrs. Ingram. He happily expected that St. Clair would get a furious letter by return express post in the morning, summoning him back to London.

It was a pity that Gyre seemed to have lost

interest in Belinda Beverley. What Perry had seen as a budding romance between the two had seemed to him added insurance that St. Clair would not be wed to Belinda.

For Belinda, the whole evening seemed to take an eternity, and when Lord Gyre announced that he and his friend Gurney would be taking their leave early in the morning, she felt her misery to be complete. She made a few half-hearted attempts to flirt with Lord St. Clair, but it was all too evident to her that he, too, was no longer interested in her. She began to long for Miss Trumble, the way a hurt child longs for its mother. Finally, she could bear it no longer and, pleading a headache, she curtsied to the company. Only Lord Gyre saw the sign of tears in her large eyes and felt a momentary weakening. Then he hardened his heart. Belinda Beverley was crying with thwarted ambition, that was all.

When Belinda at last climbed sadly into bed, she heard Lizzie's light step come along the corridor and pause outside the door. Belinda shut her eyes tightly, prepared to feign sleep, not able to bear the thought of Lizzie's probable recriminations.

But Lizzie went on her way to her own room. Belinda gave a shaky sob. Lizzie had no doubt decided that her sister was such a failure that there was no use talking to her any more.

*   *   *

Belinda awoke early but forced herself back to sleep, reluctant to face the new day. When she awoke again it was to hear that the house was in an unusual bustle. She climbed down from the high bed and looked down at the front of the house. Carriages were drawn up at the front door and luggage was being loaded into the rumble of each.

She rang the bell for her maid. 'Is everyone leaving, Betty?' she demanded.

'Oh, yes, miss. My lord do be in such a taking.'

'Saint Clair?'

'Yes, miss. He received a letter by the post-boy and he started shouting that he must leave, that we all must leave.'

'How odd. Where is Lizzie?'

At that moment, the door opened and Lizzie came in. 'What a coil!' she exclaimed. 'Lord Saint Clair's father is in a taking. Lord Saint Clair punched Mr. Vane on the nose and called him a tattle-tale, and Mr. Vane blacked Saint Clair's eye, and Mr. Burke and Lord Gyre separated them. It seems that Mr. Vane wrote to the earl, Saint Clair's father, to say that Saint Clair was becoming enamoured of Mrs. Ingram.'

'Mrs. Ingram!'

'Yes, Mrs. Ingram,' said Lizzie with a flash of contempt. 'While you were dallying with Lord Gyre, Mrs. Ingram was trying to secure the prize. It is as well for you, Belinda, that she is a

Fallen Woman and not marriageable.'

Lady Beverley came in, her face a mask of petulance. 'It is too bad,' she mourned. 'I explained to Saint Clair that I could not be rushed about in this hurly-burly fashion and I could run Mannerling for him in his absence, and he rudely told me that my own home was hard by and suggested I go to it.'

'And that is a very good idea, too,' said Belinda, who longed again to speak to Miss Trumble.

'And let Saint Clair slip through your fingers, Belinda? Fustian. I will summon up all the weak strength the Good Lord has left me to do what is right for my daughter. Get servants to attend to our packing, Betty, and quickly, too. With any luck we may be able to share the same post-house as Saint Clair on the road to London, and Belinda may there try to attract him.'

The door was standing open and Belinda, looking over her mother's shoulder, saw Lord Gyre going past. She hoped he had not heard her mother's last remark but was gloomily sure that he had.

*   *   *

Miss Trumble learned of the departure of the house party because Lord Gyre, despite Gurney Burke's protests, felt somehow obliged to stop at Brookfield House and tell her.

uncle.'

'Pooh,' muttered Lizzie and would not be comforted.

Even the sight of the racing curricle which Lord Gyre had borrowed from the stables to drive them or the appearance of the handsome marquess himself in impeccable morning coat and snowy cravat did little to cheer her.

They drove the short distance to Brookfield House. Miss Trumble herself came out to meet them, her face breaking into a glad smile of welcome. Lord Gyre saw an elderly lady whose curls were still glossy brown and with fine eyes in a wrinkled face.

Belinda flew into her arms, crying, 'We are come! We have missed you so much.'

Lizzie followed reluctantly.

Belinda introduced Lord Gyre and then said gaily, 'Miss Trumble was at that musicale where we first met.'

Lord Gyre remembered only that Belinda's companion on that evening had been a lady with puffed-out cheeks and a ferocious black wig and assumed Belinda had made a mistake.

'The day is fine,' said Miss Trumble. 'We will take tea in the garden. You must see Barry.'

At that moment the odd man came around the corner of the house. Lord Gyre had heard much gossip about the haughtiness and pride of the Beverleys, but there was no sign of it as even little Lizzie greeted this servant like an old friend.

eyes and he visibly preened.

Good heavens, thought Mrs. Ingram, amused. Would it not put the cat among the pigeons were I to attract this amiable fool? I would be saving the beautiful Belinda from herself. But we'll see . . . we'll see.

*   *   *

Now that the novelty of being back at Mannerling was over, Lady Beverley relapsed into one of her mysterious illnesses. She had become all too accustomed to the invalid state, lying on a day-bed and keeping the servants running hither and thither to fetch things for her. And so she did not know her two youngest daughters were to visit their home with Lord Gyre. Belinda had behaved very prettily to St. Clair after dinner the evening before. Lady Beverley considered Mannerling as good as hers. She never stopped for a moment to consider that if Belinda did marry St. Clair, she might not want her mother in residence.

Lizzie was inclined to sulk as she went down to the great hall with Belinda. She feared her sister was going to neglect St. Clair in favour of Gyre. Belinda looked at her pinched face, half in exasperation and half in amusement. Only the mad Beverleys would fear a marriage to a rich and handsome marquess. 'Gyre is simply being kind,' she assured Lizzie. 'He is so much older than I am. He goes on rather like an

Mrs. Ingram found herself walking with St. Clair. 'You are a hero,' she said in her light, amused voice. 'But does it not alarm you that someone deliberately tried to drown you?'

'Might have been a prank,' said St. Clair. 'I mean, chaps will play pranks. We once sawed through old Lord Eaner's carriage floor, just enough, you know. Carriage sets off, floor gives way, old boy running like mad. We laughed ourselves silly.'

'He could have been killed, you wicked man!'

St. Clair beamed at her with approval. He found he liked being called wicked. 'Oh, I'm a bit of a rip,' he said complacently. A faint elusive scent was coming from her clothes. Her bosom was deep and generous. He felt an unaccustomed stirring of physical interest. Women usually frightened him. A few brief nasty tumbles in brothels had left him with an extreme distaste of sex.

'What think you of my waistcoat?' he asked suddenly.

Mrs. Ingram studied the waistcoat. It was a gaudy creation of sky-blue silk embroidered with sunflowers.

'The pink of fashion,' she commented.

'You think so? I say, I am glad you are here. It is pleasant to have the company of a mature lady of discernment.'

'Why, thank you, my lord.' Mrs. Ingram flashed him a coquettish look from her fine

'Has anything gone wrong?' she asked.

Now Gurney regarded this governess as a servant and expected his friend to give some bland reason, but to his surprise Lord Gyre told Miss Trumble exactly why St. Clair had been summoned to London.

'Mrs. Ingram,' said Miss Trumble thoughtfully. 'Why, that might answer very well.'

'What can you mean?' demanded Gurney haughtily.

'Only that she is a rich and mature lady of good sense and Lord Saint Clair's mother died when he was young and I think he needs a lady to look after him.'

'I cannot think that Earl Durbridge would countenance such an alliance,' said Gurney. 'He wants his son to marry, not take a mistress.'

'I was thinking of marriage,' said Miss Trumble equably.

'As we are being so open,' said Gurney, 'may I point out that Belinda Beverley's ambition is to marry Saint Clair herself?'

'Oh, Belinda will come to her senses soon enough,' said the governess, 'if she has not already done so.'

'Miss Belinda has come to her senses enough to realize that if she marries Gyre, then she believes she can get him to buy her Mannerling.'

'I am sure you are mistaken. Are you sure you overheard her conversation with Lizzie correctly, Mr. Burke? Listening at doors is not always a reliable way of gaining information.'

Gurney turned red. 'I do not listen at doors,' he said wrathfully. 'This was an odd case. I decided my friend needed protection.'

Miss Trumble's eyes glinted as she surveyed the powerful figure of the marquess. 'Yes, he does look in need of protection.'

Lord Gyre laughed. 'There is something about that house, I must admit, that twists everything and everybody. So do you leave for London, Miss Trumble?'

'Yes, I will go tomorrow. There are still things to do here.'

*   *   *

'It's your own fault,' said Mirabel Dauncey crossly as St. Clair's well-sprung travelling-carriage swayed along the London road. 'What were you about, flirting with that Ingram woman? You handed Perry his revenge on a plate.'

'She understands me,' said St. Clair moodily.

'A whore's trick.'

'You say anything insulting about Mrs. Ingram and you are no longer my friend, Mirabel.'

'I apologize. But there was the Chalmers chit. All you had to do was drop the handkerchief, delight your pa, and spike Perry's guns. Before you even see the old man,

124

you should go round to the Beverleys and propose. Then Perry will be left high and dry.'

'I'll think about it,' said St. Clair sulkily.

*   *   *

Mrs. Ingram looked out at the passing landscape and wondered whether to carry on with the game or let it drop. But the thought of letting Perry Vane make all the running went against the grain. She was sure she could ingratiate herself with Earl Durbridge. But how? He was hardly going to ask her to tea. As it approached evening, she let down the glass and leaned out. They were approaching The Pelican, a posting-house where they were to stay the night, and as her carriage swung in under the arched entrance, she saw St. Clair's carriage being led off to the stables.

Her eyes gleamed. She suddenly thought of a way of spiting Perry.

She learned that St. Clair and his friend Mirabel were dining in a private parlour and decided to dine herself first before making a move. She debated whether to send her maid, Agnes, to St. Clair's room with a note summoning him. But he might be sharing a bedchamber with Mirabel Dauncey and Mirabel might talk him out of seeing her.

'Agnes,' she said, 'do go and find out discreetly if Lord Saint Clair has his own room or if he is sharing it with Mr. Dauncey.'

125

'And I think madam should go to bed and get a proper night's sleep,' said Agnes with all the freedom of speech of an old servant.

'Do as you are told!' snapped Mrs. Ingram.

After about fifteen minutes, Agnes returned and said crossly that Lord St. Clair was in the Nelson Room and Mr. Dauncey in the room next door, the Trafalgar.

'Thank you, Agnes, you may retire. I will put myself to bed.'

Agnes opened her mouth to say something and then obviously decided against it. Mrs. Ingram sat by the window to wait. She waited until the noisy sounds from the taproom below began to diminish and a few drunken good-nights echoed along the old corridors of the posting-house.

Then she sat down at the toilet-table and brushed her thick red hair down on her shoulders, then applied make-up with a skilful hand, finishing by rouging her lips. Then, draping a brightly coloured shawl about her shoulders, she made her way out and along the corridor, checking the names of each room on the brass plates nailed to the door of each. When she reached the Nelson, she pressed her ear to the door to make sure Mirabel was not in there.

After a few moments, she scratched at the door. There was no reply. She tried the door handle. The door was locked. She was about to give up, but the sound of someone ascending

126

the staircase prompted her to further action. She hammered on the room—loudly.

'Who's there?' demanded a voice from within the room.

'It is I, Mrs. Ingram.'

She heard him grumble and then the door swung open. He blinked a little at the vision that was Mrs. Ingram with her hair down.

'Let me in,' urged Mrs. Ingram, 'someone is coming.'

He stood aside and she slipped into the room. He closed the door. She put her bed candle down on the toilet-table.

Saint Clair, wrapped in a gaudy dressing-gown, eyed her suspiciously, seeing her now as the reason he was in the suds.

'I came to help you,' said Mrs. Ingram calmly.

'You can't help me.' Saint Clair sat down on the edge of the bed. 'No one can help me. That damned Perry has informed on me and my father has summoned me.'

'And you are rushing to see him as soon as you get to London?'

'Got to. Else he will disinherit me and give all to Perry.'

'That would be a mistake. Do you not think it would be better if someone interceded for you first? Someone who could tell your father that there was nothing in it?'

'You mean Mirabel?'

'No, that would not answer. You gave me the

127

impression that your father does not approve of your friends. Mr. Dauncey is not exactly persuasive—but I am.'

'You!' said St. Clair rudely. 'You're the reason I am being called back.'

'Exactly. And therefore I am exactly the person to persuade your father that you were on the point of proposing to Belinda Beverley and would have done so had not Mr. Vane's malice stopped you from doing so.'

'But he would not receive you!'

'He must leave the house sometimes. Where does he go?'

'To his club. White's.'

'I can hardly go there. Nowhere else?'

'Yes, he rides in the Row at nine o'clock every morning.'

'Then you must delay your journey back by one day, that is all, and leave things to me.'

Saint Clair looked at her. 'But what will you do when you introduce yourself and he simply rides off?'

'He will not ride off. Trust me. But you must not tell any of this to Mr. Dauncey. A charming man, but he has neither your wit nor intelligence, my lord.'

Saint Clair visibly preened. The longing to have matters smoothed for him before he saw his father was beginning to make him look on Mrs. Ingram as a saviour.

'Simply tell Mr. Dauncey that you need to gather your strength before facing your father and wish to reside here one more day.'

'I can do that. Demme, I have nothing to lose.'

'I am sure your father has heard nothing of the damaged rowing-boat. I could of course portray it as an attempt on your life.'

'That might get his sympathy.'

'And then I could tell him that Lord Gyre and everyone suspected Mr. Vane of doing the damage.'

'Oh, famous! Wondrous! If only I could see my father angry with his sainted Perry just the once!'

'You will . . . if you will be guided by me. And now I must go to bed.'

She curtsied to him formally, knowing instinctively that to flirt with him at this point would frighten him away.

*   *   *

The next day Mirabel listened suspiciously as St. Clair airily said he had decided to rack up at the posting-house for another night.

'Shouldn't you ought to press on to your father's and get it over with?' demanded Mirabel.

'Give the old man time to cool off.'

'And Perry Vane time to drip more poison in his ear!'

Saint Clair wavered and then said firmly, 'I know what I'm doing, and if you don't like it, get your own carriage and go on to London.'

'I saw that Ingram woman leaving this morning,' said Mirabel. 'Didn't speak to her, did you?'

'Not I. I'm in deep enough trouble already.'

* * *

The following morning, followed by his groom, Earl Durbridge was trotting along Rotten Row on his mare, Sally, when he saw an elegant lady on a black stallion approaching, also at a sedate trot, from the other direction. As they came abreast, she suddenly swayed in the saddle and put a hand up to her forehead.

'Whoa!' cried the earl, reining in his horse. 'Are you all right, madam?'

With an expertise amazing in a fainting woman, she reined in her own horse after backing it so that she and the earl were side by side.

'I think I will dismount,' she said weakly. 'I feel a trifle dizzy.'

'Where is your groom?'

'The silly man is about somewhere,' said Mrs. Ingram, looking about her vaguely. 'No matter, I will dismount myself.'

'Can't have that,' said the earl gallantly. He called to his groom to hold their horses' heads and then assisted Mrs. Ingram from the saddle.

'I thank you,' she said. 'I should not have gone riding after so much recent travel.'

'I think we should introduce ourselves,' he said bracingly. 'I am Durbridge.'

To his consternation, this attractive woman looked at him in shock, and then, drooping her head, began to sob bitterly.

'My stars, ma'am. Whatever can be the matter? Come now. There is a bench over there where we may sit down until you recover yourself.'

Once they were seated, Mrs. Ingram looked at him with eyes swimming with tears. She did hope the earl would not notice the strong smell of onion juice coming from the handkerchief which she clutched in her hand.

'My lord,' said Mrs. Ingram, throwing back her head, 'I regret to tell you that I am Mrs. Ingram.'

He half-rose, his face becoming mottled with anger. But her next words stopped him. 'Yes, I am the one that your nephew, Mr. Vane, most cruelly used to put you against your own son after his attempt to kill him failed.'

The earl slowly sat down again and gazed at her open-mouthed, like a stuffed pike.

'What is ... what are you ... what the deuce are you talking about?'

So she told him about the rowing-boat and about how the house party had joked about Mr. Vane's obsession with Mannerling, and how they had all ceased joking when they became aware that Mr. Vane was prepared to go to quite considerable lengths to discredit St. Clair.

'And so your son turned to me, a lady old enough to be his mother,' said Mrs. Ingram in a low voice. She was only eight years older than St. Clair. 'I immediately said that he must go straight to you and tell you of Vane's perfidy, but he said you would shout at him and would not believe him.'

'And why should I believe *you*, madam?'

'You do not have to. You have only to speak to the Marquess of Gyre. He examined the rowing-boat and found it had been deliberately damaged.'

'But Gyre would back your story because it's well known that ... harrumph!'

'You mean it is well-known that I once had an affair with Gyre? I had a very unhappy marriage, my lord. My late husband was a brute.'

And that, thought Mrs. Ingram bitterly, was nothing but the truth.

'When he died and I was out of mourning, my freedom went to my head. I had a brief liaison with Gyre, and only Gyre. The marquess urged me to be discreet, but I somehow felt by behaving disgracefully, I was getting my revenge on Ingram. But there were other people there at the house party who will confirm my story. It is my belief that your son was on the point of proposing marriage to Belinda Beverley when your letter, summoning him back to London, arrived. I have been very frank with you, my lord, and I do not like discussing my private life with anyone. I feel that due to one unfortunate affair I have been unfairly damned as a member of the demi-monde and yet, you should know, if I really were, I would not be invited to the best houses, and I go everywhere, even to Almack's. I simply do not see why the ambitions—evil ambitions—of your nephew should be so transparent to everyone but you, my lord, for I can see you are a shrewd man of honour and intelligence.'

'I will reserve judgement,' said the earl slowly, 'until I have seen Toby.'

'Before you see Lord Saint Clair, why do you not see Mr. Vane and, armed with the information I have given you, try to look at him with new eyes and see what you can see?'

'I will do that, madam. I owe my son that much. But Toby Saint Clair has always been useless and foppish.'

'He has not your strength of character, my lord, but then few young men these days do.'

'You have the right of it. Well, well, do not distress yourself further.'

Mrs. Ingram gave him a dazzling smile. 'Your son is most fond of you, are you aware of that?'

'So he should be,' said the earl, amazed. 'I'm his father, ain't I?'

*   *   *

Perry Vane waited eagerly for the earl to return

from his morning's ride. He rubbed his hands together nervously. He felt Mannerling was as good as his. He could hear the wide quiet rooms and long green lawns calling to him. He felt like a man who had been temporarily separated from the love of his life.

At last he heard the bustle below stairs which heralded the earl's return. Soon the door of the earl's study, where Perry was waiting, was flung open and the earl strode in.

'Oh, it's you, is it?' he snapped.

Perry meekly dropped his eyes. 'I am distressed I had to send you that letter about Toby, but it was imperative you knew what was going on before that harpy got him in her clutches.'

'I happen to be acquainted with Mrs. Ingram and think her a fine lady.'

Perry's eyelids blinked rapidly. 'But, my lord, she is much older than your son, and her reputation—'

'Enough! I am more interested in why the rowing-boat my son was in sank, and why it showed all signs of having been tampered with.'

'I know nothing of that.'

'I also want to know why it is that everyone except me seems to know that your sole aim is to discredit Toby and get Mannerling for yourself.'

It was the age of sensibility, and so Perry decided the only sensible thing to do was to burst into tears. This was not difficult for him for he was upset and outraged. He could feel Mannerling swirling away from him. It should belong to him, not to some useless fop who would run that glorious place into the ground.

'Come now, boy, dry your tears,' said the earl gruffly. 'Perhaps I have been too harsh.'

Perry dried his eyes and said in a choked voice, 'Have I not always tried to serve you? You have always praised my common sense. Would I do such a childish thing as to damage a rowing-boat that I did not even know your son would be in? Do you think I tried to *drown* him with so many servants and guests around?'

The earl frowned. Mrs. Ingram had been most persuasive. And whom should he find to corroborate her strange story? Gyre had been her lover, so he would surely agree with her. Belinda Beverley and those other Beverleys would probably agree because their ambition was to get Mannerling, and so they would only be interested in the owner. Mirabel Dauncey was his son's friend and would say anything he wanted; Gurney Burke was a friend of Gyre. There were Miss Chalmers and her mother, and the Hartley twins and their parents. Perhaps it would be as well to reserve judgement until he had talked to either the Hartleys or the Chalmers.

'I will wait and see,' said the earl. 'You may go.'

'When did you meet Mrs. Ingram?' asked Perry.

'Oh, some time ago,' said the earl, not wanting to say he had only met the lady for the first time that morning, or Perry might think she had deliberately engineered the meeting. The earl was beginning to think that perhaps she had.

*   *   *

Saint Clair mounted the stairs to his father's study later that day, feeling as if his Hessian boots were weighted down with lead. He had planned to leave 'the old man' to simmer for another day, but he felt he could no longer enjoy himself with the thought of the row to come hanging over him.

He was told his father was having his afternoon nap, and so he was forced to kick his heels in the study for over an hour while he wondered whether it might be possible to die from an excess of fright.

At last he heard the shuffle of his father's slippers approaching the door and stood up.

'Turned up at last, hey?' growled the earl, slumping down into his favourite armchair. 'Sit down, sit down, and stop standing there goggling at me.'

Saint Clair did as he was bid. His legs felt like jelly and his mouth was dry. He had been so upset at the thought of the interview that he had not painted his face and was—for him—soberly dressed.

Pity the boy takes after Jenny, thought the earl, thinking without much affection of his late wife, who always seemed to burst into tears whenever she saw him.

'So what's this I hear from Perry about you romancing that Mrs. Ingram?'

'I was not romancing her. She is a kind and sympathetic lady.' And then fright sharpened St. Clair's not normally agile brain and he added, 'After I had to rescue Miss Chalmers from the lake when we were nearly both drowned, I realized someone had been trying to kill me, and everyone began to look like a villain.'

If St. Clair had blamed Perry, his statement would not have made such an impression on the earl and somehow St. Clair had sensed that.

'The fact is that I met this Mrs. Ingram by accident in the Park this morning, m'boy, and she told me all about your brave rescue.' The thought that this feckless son of his had actually rescued anyone gave the earl a warm glow and he began to return as well to his earlier opinion that Mrs. Ingram was a fine woman. 'But who in that house party would want to injure you?' asked the earl.

Saint Clair longed to say, 'Perry, of course,' but somehow a new cunning had entered his brain. He considered Perry a slimy creature. Instead, he raised his buckram-wadded shoulders in a shrug. 'Blessed if I know. I mean,

137

who would have anything to gain by my death? You may think I'm a poor sort of chap, but fact is, people don't take violent dislikes to me.'

The earl sat brooding. He had always thought of Perry as being everything he longed his son to be—decent, reliable, and at all times respectful. He had always prided himself on being a good judge of character. He shook his head like a baffled bull. The boat had probably sprung a leak. To think of anything else was too Gothic.

'Let's get back to your marriage prospects, Toby. I thought you were going to propose to the Beverley chit.'

Saint Clair opened his mouth to say that he was going to see Lady Beverley that very day to declare his intentions, but something stopped him. A new idea that somewhere there might be a lady for him who would stir his senses had entered his mind. He decided quickly that the sensible thing would be to consult Mrs. Ingram first.

'I was going to,' he lied, 'before that near drowning addled my wits. Then I got cautious. We both know, sir, that the Beverleys want Mannerling more than anything. Well, I may be a poor sort of specimen, but I began to think I was maybe better than just a target for someone's ambitions.'

'You're not going to talk of love,' snorted the earl. 'We're both men of the world. You find yourself a suitable wife and then you get yourself a mistress; that's the way it's done.'

But the idea of having to cope with a wife *and* a mistress terrified St. Clair.

'So you actually want me to propose to Belinda Beverley?' he asked.

'Well, now, m'boy, your rescue of Miss Chalmers proves there's more backbone in you than I had previously thought. I'll give you to the end of the Season. What about the Chalmers girl, hey? Money there, good family.'

'I am learning wisdom, Pa,' said St. Clair, thinking all the time what a deuced cunning chap he was becoming. 'Don't do any harm to shop around. We're an old family, demme, a proud family. Nothing but the best for us.'

The earl's eyes glowed. 'You're right, boy. Take your time.'

And so St. Clair left, feeling like a man who had been losing heavily all night at the tables in St. James's, only to rise at dawn with his luck changed and a fortune in his pocket.

CHAPTER FIVE

But at my back I always hear
Time's wingèd chariot hurrying near.
And yonder all before us lie
Deserts of vast eternity.
Thy beauty shall no more be found;
Nor, in thy marble vault, shall sound
My echoing song: then worms shall try

That long preserved virginity:
And your quaint honour turn to dust;
And into ashes all my lust.
The grave's a fine and private place,
But none I think do there embrace.
                              —*ANDREW MARVELL*

Belinda welcomed the return to London of
Miss Trumble. Lady Beverley had quite
forgotten that she had banished the governess
to the country and was also glad to have this
maker of headache potions back again.

And now that Lord St. Clair did not call,
Lady Beverley retreated once more into
imaginary illness. Belinda's social life was
divided in two. In the afternoons, she attended
lectures and art exhibitions with Miss Trumble,
and in the evenings, she went out to balls and
parties chaperoned by her sister, Abigail.

Lord Gyre, it seemed, was nowhere. Belinda
longed to ask his whereabouts but was fearful
he would get to hear of her interest and despise
her the more. But at a breakfast party, she met
Perry Vane again.

She was seated next to him at a long table in
the garden of Mrs. Tamworth's home.
Remembering the stories of Perry's plots to
discredit St. Clair, she would have snubbed him
had he not immediately turned to her and
began to talk of Mannerling, and as he talked,
Belinda could feel all the old, sick yearning for
her former home engulfing her, a superstitious

140

feeling that somehow her life would be less bleak and empty if only she were back 'home' again.

He had an open, friendly, and easy manner, and as they talked, Belinda began to think the stories she had heard about him must have been lies. After they had been talking for some time, Perry said in a low voice, 'I was extremely upset to be falsely accused of damaging that rowing-boat. I wish my feckless cousin no harm. I was, however, concerned that he would ultimately ruin Mannerling, because he is a gambler.'

'Mannerling seems to attract gamblers,' said Belinda, thinking of her own father and another previous owner, Ajax Judd. 'Do you think the house is haunted? Mrs. Ingram had a bad fright and the servants do say that they see ghosts.'

'I think Mrs. Ingram is an over-emotional woman who likes to be the centre of attention,' he said drily, 'and the servant class likes drama.'

And all the while they talked, Perry wondered if this beautiful girl whose love of Mannerling matched his own could be of any assistance to him.

Abigail had not heard any of the stories about Perry. She saw his interest in her sister and asked about him, learning that he was Earl Durbridge's nephew, and appeared to be generally liked. Lizzie had been taken off on calls with Miss Trumble, and so Belinda was free to enjoy Perry's company.

It was almost like being back at Mannerling, she thought dreamily, as each described room after room. Perry grew more enthusiastic. He considered the gardens too formal and said he would like to see them more romantic, less *planned.*

At one point, Belinda looked down the long table and saw Gurney Burke watching her with a cynical look on his face and turned her face away. But the damage had been done. Memories of Lord Gyre flooded into her mind and she could feel a dragging weight of misery engulf her.

But during the dancing after the meal, Perry took her up for two dances. He was an undemanding and easy companion and a very good dancer. Belinda agreed to go driving with him the following day, and set her mind to forgetting all about Lord Gyre and her failure to attract St. Clair.

*   *   *

'What are you doing here?' Lord Gyre asked Gurney later that day, after Gurney had strolled into the coffee-room at White's. 'I thought you were enjoying yourself at the Tamworths' breakfast.'

'I find these affairs increasingly tedious,' said Gurney, sinking into a chair opposite the marquess which creaked under his weight.

'Food bad?'

'No, food excellent, company dull. Perry Vane was there, much enamoured with that scheming creature, Belinda Beverley.'

The marquess's face darkened. 'I will brook no criticism of that lady, whatever I myself might think of her schemes.'

'Well, she has met a soul mate in Perry,' said Gurney sulkily. 'So, are you still planning to repair to the country tomorrow?'

Lord Gyre opened his mouth to say that, yes, he would be going, but he had a sudden bright picture of Belinda Beverley laughing with Perry Vane and flirting with him. Lord Gyre distrusted Perry. Thinking back to the house party, he remembered he had been convinced that Perry had tried to sabotage that boat. Was it Belinda's fault that she was so determined to gain that wretched place, Mannerling, at all costs? She was being pushed by that mother of hers.

He himself had received an invitation to the Tamworths' breakfast. These breakfast affairs actually started at three o'clock in the afternoon and went on until dawn.

'I do not know whether I shall leave London tomorrow,' he said. 'I have a few things to attend to in Town. Now, if you will excuse me, Gurney . . .'

'Thought we might have a rubber of whist,' said Gurney. 'Besides, I have only just got here.'

The marquess smiled. 'And I, on the contrary, have been here for some time.'

Once outside the club, he told himself severely that go to to the Tamworth affair at this late hour would be folly. But if Perry Vane was suddenly showing an interest in Belinda Beverley, then it could hardly be for love.

Still chastising himself on his folly, he returned to his town house, changed into his dress clothes, and set out for the Tamworths' home.

Belinda, with a supreme effort, had put thoughts about him, St. Clair, and Mannerling out of her mind. Perry had already danced with her twice and could not dance with her again without occasioning comment. But she found she had a new worry to occupy her mind. The army captain who had taken her up for the supper dance proved to be extremely drunk. It was the waltz and several times he had stood on her toes, quite painfully.

The Marquess of Gyre entered the conservatory where the dancing was being held in time to see the captain trip once more over Belinda's feet and stretch his length on the floor. He moved forward quickly. 'My dance, I think,' he said, putting his arm about her waist and sweeping her away while the captain was helped from the floor by his friends.

'Thank you,' said Belinda when she could.

'My pleasure.' He felt himself growing angry.

She was pliant in his arms, and the light scent she wore assailed his senses. They completed the rest of the dance in silence. He led her into the supper-room. Perry watched them moodily and then was surprised to experience a pang of pure jealousy. Somehow, Belinda Beverley had become entwined in his mind with Mannerling. He had even begun to dream about the two of them enjoying the glories of the place as man and wife.

'So here we are together again,' said the marquess lightly, steering Belinda to the end of one of the long tables so that he might be more private with her. 'I see that churl, Perry Vane, is here.'

'I found Mr. Vane a sympathetic companion,' said Belinda defiantly.

'Oho! What is the scheme now? Is Mr. Vane so confident of ingratiating himself with Durbridge to the detriment of Saint Clair that he feels he will get Mannerling?'

'Nothing like that, my lord. You see plots everywhere.'

'You have been open with me about your own plots and stratagems. Why should I not see plots everywhere?'

'Do not bait me, my lord,' said Belinda fiercely. 'I have decided to enjoy my Season. Saint Clair is not interested in me.'

'I must ask you this, for it has been troubling me. We have fallen into the way of being blunt with each other. My friend Gurney overheard you planning to entrap me and then ask me to buy you Mannerling. You were talking with your sister in the morning-room at Mannerling.'

Belinda blushed furiously. 'It was a joke!'

'And was it also a joke when you said you could have me any time you liked?'

She gazed at him in furious surprise. 'I never said such a thing. Why did you believe your friend so easily? Why did you not just *ask?*'

'I am asking you now.'

'What Mr. Burke heard was a joke I was sharing with my sister. My sister and my mother are very ambitious on my behalf. I was anxious to return to my old role of saviour of the family fortunes and to protect myself from criticism and recriminations. You had your revenge. You ignored me and Saint Clair appeared smitten with Mrs. Ingram, and so I became the family disgrace.'

He waved his hand to encompass the room. 'There are many attractive and decent men at the Season. Why cannot you behave like the other débutantes and concentrate on securing an honourable marriage?'

'And why cannot you mind your own business?' she flashed back at him. 'My concerns are none of your concern, my lord.'

'You have the right of it. And yet I feel I should warn you against the Honourable Peregrine Vane.'

'Why? Did Mr. Burke overhear some of his

conversation as well and give you a highly coloured and distorted account of it?'

'No, I am relying entirely on my own observation.'

'And yet you did not do so in my case!'

'I did. You admit to being a scheming minx, Belinda Beverley.'

'What an exasperating man you are! I wish I had never been so open with you.'

'And yet that is part of your charm.'

She blushed again. 'Come now,' he said gently. 'Drink your wine and eat your food and let us talk about something else. How goes the estimable Miss Trumble?'

'Miss Trumble is something of a mystery.'

His eyes mocked her. 'Miss Trumble? Never!'

'You see, Mama is often not well enough to escort us to functions, and if Miss Trumble has to do so, she disguises herself in a frightful wig as if she fears to be recognized.'

'Perhaps she is the disgraced member of an aristocratic family?'

'No, I think she is merely a trifle eccentric. Such a stalwart as our Miss Trumble cannot have anything too sinister in her past.'

'How did your mother come to employ her?'

'My mother advertised for a governess and all seemed to be unsuitable until Miss Trumble turned up, complete with luggage, accepted the post and settled in. She did not have any references, but after some time she produced them and they were impeccable.'

He laughed. 'There is probably some previous employer abroad in society whom she detests. She does not want to be recognized by her. What does Miss Trumble think of your ambitions?'

'My former ambitions, my lord. Well, to be sure, she is heartily tired of the Beverley ambitions to retrieve Mannerling.' And now that she was beside him again, Belinda had forgotten all about Perry and all about Mannerling.

'Sensible woman! Are you now telling me that all hope is really gone?'

'It was all very silly, really,' said Belinda. 'I am not going to spoil the rest of the Season by worrying about it.'

Some imp prompted her to add, 'So who do you suggest I should set my cap at now?'

'I do not know,' he said rather tetchily. 'I am sure your sister, Lady Burfield, and the excellent Miss Trumble are armed with lists of eligibles.'

'Then I must begin to study them.'

'I am only sorry I shall not be in London for the rest of the Season that I might witness your triumphs,' he said, and all the heady elation Belinda had been beginning to feel died away and she said in a small voice, 'You are leaving? Why?' She tried to rally and added, 'Are you not looking for a bride?'

'Not I. So far I have never come across

anyone suitable.'

'You must set very high standards.'

'Believe me, Miss Belinda, I do.'

'Then I must say goodbye to you. I doubt if we shall meet again.'

'What? Will you not send me an invitation to your wedding?'

'Oh, gladly, my lord. I did not think you would wish to attend.'

'If you marry such as Perry Vane, I might not.'

'Perhaps I might. I feel you are mistaken in him.'

'Why do I trouble myself? Your follies are your own affair.'

'Exactly,' said Belinda.

She picked morosely at her food and he studied her downcast face. The supper-room was emptying. The dancing had started up again. He felt he should leave, but then she had barely eaten anything.

'So do you plan to see Mr. Vane again?' he asked at last.

'We are to go driving together tomorrow.'

'My dear widgeon! Is Perry Vane the best you can do?'

'I repeat, I find him undemanding and amiable company.'

'Meaning you have found someone to talk to about Mannerling, over and over again?'

'Oh, leave me alone,' said Belinda, exasperated and on the point of tears. Her voice trembled. 'You seem determined to find fault with me.'

'There, I apologize. Do you go to the opera tomorrow night?'

'Yes, my sister has a box.'

'Then I will delay going to the country and escort you.'

'Why do you think I would relish your company?' demanded Belinda.

'Because I am the fashion and any interest I might show in you will draw suitors to your side.'

'You are vain!'

'I am ever practical and pragmatic.'

Belinda opened her mouth to tell him that she did not want to be escorted by him, but somehow the thought that he would be leaving London made her say in a little voice, 'Oh, very well. I will go with you.'

'You are supposed to be thrown into a flutter of gratification and say, "Oh, my lord, I am so honoured."'

She suddenly let out an endearing giggle and her large eyes flirted up at him and she said with a simper, 'Oh, my lord, I am so honoured.'

'That's better,' he said, although his heart beat harder, that heart which he had always called his own.

Abigail entered the supper-room, which was now empty except for the pair of them, looking anxious. Gyre's attentions to Belinda were flattering, but to remain at her side in an empty supper-room was too much, and unless he meant to propose marriage to her, his monopolizing of her would disaffect other possible suitors.

'The dancing has started again,' said Abigail lightly.

The marquess stood up. 'May I have the honour of escorting your sister to the opera tomorrow night?'

'Certainly,' said Abigail, surprised and gratified. Her little sister was doing well— driving with Mr. Vane, who had already secured her permission, in the afternoon and being escorted in the evening by Gyre.

'After that, I shall be leaving for the country,' said Lord Gyre, 'and will not be back in London for some time.'

'Then the social scene will be lessened by your absence,' said Abigail, very glad now she had interrupted them, since Gyre did not seem to have any serious feelings about Belinda. It was only a pity that Lord St. Clair appeared to have lost interest in her.

* * *

At that very moment, Lord St. Clair was cosily ensconced in Mrs. Ingram's drawing-room. He had called to proffer his thanks over her intervention with his father and then had found himself reluctant to leave.

'I feel like getting even with Perry,' said St.

Clair. 'But he's a cunning one. If only I could get him to show his hand.'

Mrs. Ingram looked at him measuringly. She was becoming increasingly fond of this amiable fop. 'If you want to rile him, you could say you think Mannerling has too much land and you intend to sell some of it off as soon as you are married.'

'But he'll go running to Pa!'

'No, I somehow do not think so. He knows you have only to deny it and accuse him of trying to discredit you. And what proof will he have, since you don't intend to sell the land anyway?'

Saint Clair's pale eyes gleamed with excitement. 'What do you think he would do?'

'I think he might try something drastic. You would need to be on your guard. Don't you remember the scandal about Harvey Brooks, who wanted his brother's inheritance? He sent his brother a box of poisoned chocolates. Brother feeds one first to the family dog, which promptly drops dead. Runners call at the shop where the chocolates were purchased and found they were purchased by none other than Harvey Brooks. It was hushed up because the family did not want an open scandal, and so Harvey was shipped to America to join all the other murderers and poisoners. If I ever went to America, I should be quite terrified to accept an invitation to dinner!'

'Oh, I don't think he would go that far.'

152

'I think he might. And if your father thought your life was in danger, I really think he would be prepared to give you what you want.'

Lord St. Clair looked at the ceiling and then at the floor and then, summoning up all his courage, he said, 'I want you.'

She looked at him with affection and then said, 'We'll see. But I would seek out Perry and tell him about the planned sale and see what happens. He is actually not very clever, but he thinks he is and that is his weakness.'

'No one is as clever as you, ma'am.'

'Why, thank you, sir. And now you must go or my doubtful reputation will become even more doubtful.'

He got to his feet and said to throatily, 'May I have a kiss?'

She rose as well. 'Come here.'

He walked into her arms and held her close, feeling her warm lips against his own, comforting and caressing, and he wanted her more than anything else in the world.

*　　*　　*

The next day, Perry was dressing when he found to his surprise that St. Clair had called. 'Show him up,' he said to his manservant.

He did not turn around when his cousin entered the room. He did not have to. The cloud of scent which surrounded St. Clair's body always advertised his arrival.

153

'What do you want?' demanded Perry ungraciously.

'Lot of land at Mannerling,' said St. Clair, slumping into a chair and admiring the glossy toes of his boots.

'Yes, and in very good heart, too.'

'Which means I should get a good price for it. Came to get your advice on how much I should ask.'

'You cannot sell any of the Mannerling lands!' cried Perry, his face flaming with shock and rage.

'Course I can. It's mine, ain't it?'

'Let's see what your father has to say about this.'

'Going to run to him, Mr. Tattle-Tale, are you? Well, for the moment, I'll say you're making it up to spite me. But when I'm wed, I'll do as I please.'

'Never!' shouted Perry.

'You cannot do anything about it,' said St. Clair with a truly awful smirk.

Perry fought to control his temper. He must plot, he must plan.

Then his face cleared and he said evenly, 'But you ain't married and you're not likely to be.'

Saint Clair was certainly not going to mention Mrs. Ingram. 'You're wrong,' he said. 'All I have to do is ask Belinda Beverley and she'll say yes.'

Perry had been indulging in dreams of being

154

wed to Belinda, a fellow enthusiast when it came to Mannerling. Although he had been alarmed to mark how much time Gyre had spent with Belinda the night before, he had comforted himself with the thought that everyone knew Gyre was due to leave for the country. He would propose to Belinda Beverley himself that very afternoon.

To St. Clair's surprise, his cousin, so enraged only a moment before, now began to look quite cheerful.

He hoped it was an act.

* * *

Perry drove Belinda in the Park late that afternoon. He decided to find out tentatively if he had a chance with her before approaching her mother. So he broke away from the throng in the circle and drove across the grass and reined in his team under a stand of trees.

'What are we doing here?' asked Belinda.

'Do not be alarmed,' said Perry. 'I have something important to discuss with you. Saint Clair is threatening to sell off some of the Mannerling lands.'

'He cannot!' Belinda turned quite pale.

'I agree he must be stopped. The only way he will get the earl's approval to do as he pleases with Mannerling will be if he marries. Now, the only lady who is likely to accept him is you yourself.'

155

'Then I shall refuse.'

'Miss Beverley, dear Miss Beverley, Earl Durbridge will soon become weary of Toby Saint Clair and his antics and Mannerling will be mine—and yours, too—if you would marry me.'

Belinda quickly cast down her eyes. She was suddenly frightened of Perry. She remembered Mrs. Ingram's warning that Perry was out to get Mannerling. Gyre had warned her of the same thing only the evening before.

'Your proposal is very flattering, sir,' she said. 'You are supposed to approach my mother first, you know, to ask permission to pay your addresses. But it is as well you spoke to me first. I have no longer any interest in Mannerling.'

'But only last night—'

'I have come to my senses. I cannot let my life be ruled by a mere house.'

'Mannerling is not a mere house.'

'Shall we return, Mr. Vane? I am sorry to reject your flattering proposal, but reject it I must.'

'It's Gyre, isn't it?' he demanded wrathfully.

'I am heart-free at the moment, sir, and glad of it. Now are you going to drive me home, or do I have to get down and walk?'

Perry drove her home in furious silence.

Belinda went immediately on her return to seek out Miss Trumble. She sat down and told her all that had happened.

When she had finished, Miss Trumble sat in silence for a few moments. Then she said, 'I have a little story to tell you.' She related how she had called at Mannerling before the arrival of the house party and what she had overheard Perry saying to the footman. 'But the thing that puzzles me is Saint Clair's intention to sell some of the Mannerling lands.'

'Why? He is a greedy fop.'

'A fop, yes, but greedy, no. Besides, even thinking about selling land causes some mental effort, and I would have thought Saint Clair too easygoing and careless a fellow to think of such a thing. Like Mr. Cater, who wanted Rachel as his bride only because he, too, was obsessed with Mannerling, Mr. Vane wants to present Mannerling with a suitable bride. This is madness, Belinda, and you must have nothing to do with it. I gather from Abigail that Gyre is to escort you to the opera this evening?'

'Yes.'

'He is a fine man. There, I will talk no more about him or you will think I am urging you to marry him. But watch out for Mr. Vane! I fear that man is dangerous.'

* * *

Another clever woman was listening to a tale about Mr. Vane at that very moment. 'He is plotting something,' said Mrs. Ingram. 'Now, if he were to propose to Belinda Beverley himself and be accepted, the earl might very well give him Mannerling as a wedding present.'

'Perhaps it might be as well then to let them get on with it,' said St. Clair.

'But there is also the fear that your father might consider Mr. Vane a more suitable heir.'

'Then what am I to do?' demanded St. Clair, clutching his pomaded hair.

'Propose to Belinda Beverley yourself.'

'But I want *you!*'

'We'll see. But let's force Mr. Vane's hand.'

'But how do I get out of marrying Belinda Beverley once I have proposed?'

And the normally intelligent and shrewd Mrs. Ingram made her first mistake. She had heard reports of Gyre's interest in Belinda at the breakfast, and remembered the way Gyre had looked at the girl at the house party.

'I think Miss Beverley will refuse you. You will then go to your father and tell him you have been turned down and your heart is broken. You will tell him that you might have been accepted except Perry no doubt had told Miss Beverley that Mannerling was as good as his.'

'But why should La Beverley refuse me? Everyone knows she is desperate to get her hands on that wretched house.'

'She is enamoured of Gyre and he of her. It is all the talk.'

'I say! So all I have to do is pop the question,

158

get refused and go and weep on Pa's shoulder.'

'Exactly.'

'I will do it tomorrow.'

The fact that she was a little jealous of Belinda for having evidently secured the heart of Lord Gyre had clouded Mrs. Ingram's judgement, but perhaps Gyre might have seriously considered marrying Belinda were it not for the disastrous evening which was to follow.

*   *   *

Lady Beverley and Lizzie only saw this rich and handsome marquess as the one who had blighted Belinda's ambition. Lizzie was almost insolent, ignoring Lord Gyre when he politely addressed her and defiantly tossing her red hair. Lady Beverley droned on about the loss of Mannerling and how they had hopes of Belinda's making a match of it with St. Clair. Lord Gyre began to suspect that there was real madness in the Beverley family. Had he had a chance to be alone with Belinda, perhaps he would have revised his opinion. But he had no opportunity, and Belinda was crushed and diminished by shame about her family.

After the opera, he said he was too tired to go to the ball. Belinda in a little voice suggested that in that case he should escort them home. He took a very formal leave of her. All the warmth and sparkle and magic had gone. He felt bleak and empty as he returned home to make his preparations for his departure for the country. Belinda cried herself to sleep.

CHAPTER SIX

Man proposes, but God disposes.
                              —*THOMAS À KEMPIS*

Dressed in his finest and feeling no end of a devil, Toby St. Clair presented himself the following afternoon at the Burfield town house and requested an audience with Lady Beverley.

Lady Beverley was lying down in a darkened bedchamber, eating chocolates, for she had decided she had a wasting illness and the chocolates were to build up her strength.

On hearing that Lord St. Clair wished to see her, she leaped to her feet, screaming for the lady's-maid, and then sending Abigail, who had run in to see what ailed her mother, to go and make sure Belinda had on her prettiest gown.

For a supposed invalid, Lady Beverley was changed and scented in record time, so frightened was she that the 'quarry' might escape. She swept into the drawing-room. There were two hectic spots of colour in her cheeks which owed nothing to rouge but all to excitement. Lord St. Clair gave such a long low scrape that his nose almost touched the carpet and Lady Beverley responded with a full court curtsy.

Saint Clair stood back and cleared his throat. 'I am come, Lady Beverley, to ask your permission to pay my addresses to your daughter.'

'Oh, my lord, we are so honoured, so very honoured.'

Saint Clair blinked at her nervously. He did not like all this enthusiasm. Still, Belinda would be sent for and Belinda would refuse him.

To his alarm, Lady Beverley asked him to be seated and then began to interrogate him on the state of his finances, what provision would be made for the children of the marriage, and so on.

At last St. Clair interrupted her by saying, ''Tis is all a bit premature, Lady Beverley, and I usually leave all boring financial matters to my lawyers. Of course, if I have called at an inconvenient time and Miss Belinda is not available, I will call some other day.'

'No!' shrieked Lady Beverley in alarm. And then, in a quieter voice, 'I will send Belinda to you.' She rose and gazed at him fondly. 'My son!'

After she had gone, St. Clair took out a lace-edged, scented cambric handkerchief and mopped his brow. All he wanted now was for this ordeal to be over. He longed to ring the bell and ask for a glass of brandy but did not dare.

At last Belinda came in.

161

She was very pale and did not look at all happy to see him. Saint Clair's spirits rose.

She hung her head as he went forward and took one of her cold hands in his own.

'Miss Beverley, Belinda,' he said, 'will you marry me?'

Belinda stood for a long moment in silence. She felt tired and weary and utterly miserable. Gyre had gone. Nothing was left now but to please her mother and do her duty.

'Thank you, my lord,' she said at last.

'Do not worry about it,' he began. 'I shall not mention this matter ag—What?'

'I accept your proposal, my lord.'

He opened and shut his mouth and let out a squeak of 'Thank you.'

The couple looked at each other miserably.

'I suppose that's that,' said St. Clair gloomily. 'When do you want to get married?'

'I do not know,' replied Belinda wretchedly. 'Some time next year, perhaps.'

Saint Clair began to gain courage. A whole year! Surely in that time Mrs. Ingram would think of a way to get him out of this mess.

Lady Beverley, Lizzie, and Abigail came in. Lady Beverley cast an anguished look of hope at her daughter's face.

'Wish us well,' said St. Clair in a hollow voice.

Miss Trumble appeared in the doorway and stood silently as Lady Beverley called for champagne.

Lizzie, watching Belinda's sad face, suddenly felt a terrible pang of guilt. She knew Belinda was wretched and would have given anything in that moment to be able to cry out to her sister to call the whole thing off before it was too late, but the fear of the scandal that such an outburst would cause kept her quiet.

Miss Trumble turned away and made her way up to the top of the house to talk to Barry.

'So she's done it,' said Barry when Miss Trumble had told him the news. 'The Beverleys will have Mannerling at last.'

'And much good may it do them.' Miss Trumble paced up and down Barry's small room, her silk skirts swishing over the sanded floor. 'I am persuaded that Belinda is in love with Gyre. What a match that would have been. What are we to do, Barry? Saint Clair is not a villain. It might work.'

'But you do not think so, miss,' said Barry.

She stopped her pacing and sat down with a sigh. 'No, I do not think so. I am going to interfere, Barry. I am going to call on Gyre.'

'I'll come with you, miss. You cannot take one of the carriages and will need to get a hack.'

'Then let us go while they are all still celebrating. Something must be done!'

But when they arrived at Lord Gyre's town house, it was to see the knocker had gone from the door and all the windows were shuttered.

A butler at a neighboring house informed

163

them that Lord Gyre had left for the country early that morning.

'So that is that,' said Miss Trumble.

'We could follow him to the country,' said Barry.

'No, I think that would be folly. Calling here was a rash act. I am old and weary and sick to death of Mannerling. Belinda will just need to get on with the life she has chosen.'

* * *

Saint Clair called on his father to tell him the 'glad' news. The earl promptly plunged into financial arrangements and marriage settlements and St. Clair could feel the prison chains of marriage beginning to weigh him down already. At last he made his escape and went straight to Mrs. Ingram.

She listened in dismay. Then she rallied. 'This should make Perry do something really rash. But what of Gyre?'

'Everyone says he's gone to the country, that he was with the Beverleys at the opera last night, looking like thunder.'

'I must find some way to get him back to Town,' said Mrs. Ingram. 'But let us first see how our Mr. Perry Vane reacts.'

* * *

Perry did not hear the news until the paper with the announcement of the betrothal appeared

164

with his morning chocolate.

He cursed and ranted and sent the cup of chocolate flying across the room.

He felt murderous.

All at once, he decided to go down to the country, to Mannerling. There he felt he could gather his wits and think what to do.

The servants at Mannerling knew him and would let him stay. There was no reason why either the earl or Toby should know where he was.

He drove hell for leather through the whole day and night, not stopping for rest, until he saw the tall iron gates of Mannerling looming up before his tired eyes.

He slowed his pace as he drove his sweating horses up the long drive bordered by lime trees. He had a tremendous feeling that he was coming home, that he belonged at Mannerling, that everything would be all right.

Cool rooms enfolded him in their embrace. The great house was quiet and peaceful.

After he had dined and slept, he awoke refreshed in the early evening. He felt he had been prey to a temporary bout of insanity.

He went out for a walk to enjoy a cheroot and to admire the lake from the Greek temple on the rise above it. The evening was very calm and still, broken only by the sleepy chirping of birds settling down for the night.

But when he finally turned and entered the great hall of Mannerling, his calm mood was abruptly shattered. The very walls somehow seemed to engulf him with rage and loss. His heart beat so hard, he clutched the banister and feared he might be going to have an apoplexy. And then a voice seemed to whisper in his brain that he was a milksop. He was handing this precious place over to a fop, a fop who would sell off the lands.

'Never!' he shouted suddenly, and the chandelier swung and tinkled above his head, first one half circle and then another.

And then he realized that Toby St. Clair would have to die.

*   *   *

Lord Gyre had not looked at the newspapers which were now stacked in a neat pile on his desk in his study.

He had ridden about his estates, checking what had to be done, pushing any thoughts of Belinda Beverley firmly to the back of his mind.

At last, he settled down one evening to catch up on the news, sitting by the library fire and throwing each newspaper on the floor beside his chair when he had finished reading all he wanted to read, which did not include any intelligence in the social columns.

At last he rose to go to bed, and as he bent down to scoop the pile of discarded newspapers from the floor, the flames from the fire illumined one which had fallen open at the social page. The name 'Beverley' seemed to leap up at him. He slowly picked up the newspaper and sat down again.

So she had finally got what she wanted, he thought bitterly. Be damned to her!

* * *

Lizzie sat at the end of Belinda's bed one morning and said anxiously, 'I cannot bear the guilt any longer, Belinda. You are marrying Saint Clair because of me.'

Belinda gave her sister a wan smile. 'I have managed to please everyone. Even Miss Trumble is silent on the matter, although I feel she is bitterly disappointed in me.'

'Oh, Belinda,' said Lizzie, her eyes filling with tears. 'That wretched house. I helped to drive Gyre away, did I not, with my bad behaviour that night at the opera?'

'Mama did her part, too,' said Belinda wearily. 'Think nothing of it.'

'But do you really want to marry him?'

Belinda turned her face away. 'I made a mistake. I cannot *bear* him now. His empty-headed chatter makes my head ache.'

Lizzie edged up the bed. 'You must cry off.'

'And you will blame me forever for losing Mannerling.'

'I was mad. I only want you to be happy again.'

'But can you imagine the scandal if I cried

167

off? Mama would go into a genuine decline.'

'Mama has been disappointed four times before this and survived.'

Belinda sat up and looked at her little sister wonderingly. 'And you would not mind?'

Lizzie hugged her. 'Not I.'

'I have played my part of simpering miss so well that Saint Clair is quite fond of me,' said Belinda slowly. 'What if I were to give him a disgust of me? Then we might both decide together that we should not suit.'

'Famous,' said Lizzie. 'When do you see him next?'

'This very afternoon. He is to take me driving.'

'What would shock him most?'

Belinda gave a slow smile. It was the first time she had smiled since the day of her engagement. 'I shall criticize his waistcoat. He will never forgive me for that!'

*   *   *

'So what am I to do?' St. Clair demanded of Mrs. Ingram for what seemed like the hundredth time. 'Belinda is all complacence, my father is in alt, and Perry hasn't made a move; in fact, he sent a damned expensive present.'

Mrs. Ingram was beginning to wonder if she herself was exactly what she had damned Perry Vane for being—someone who was vulnerable

168

because they thought they were clever while not being clever at all.

Then she said, 'You must give her a disgust of you.'

'How? She wants that damned house so much that I could walk all over her face with my boots on and she would only simper and say, "Why, what pretty boots, my lord."'

'Try.'

'Give me a kiss and I will try anything.'

*　　　*　　　*

Lady Beverley waved from the window as Belinda and Lord St. Clair drove off that afternoon.

Lord St. Clair was searching his mind for something really rude to say when his fair partner suddenly declared testily, 'Your horses are too showy and you do not have them properly under control.'

He goggled at her, his face flaming. 'I assure you, I can drive to an inch.'

'Stop staring at me, and pay attention to your team,' snapped Belinda.

He was so taken aback, he could not think of anything to say. He drove in a sulky silence.

When they entered the Park, Belinda took a deep breath and said in that same shrewish tone, 'We must really do something about your clothes, my lord.'

He jerked on the reins and his horses reared.

His tiger jumped down from the back and ran to their heads and got them under control.

'What did you say?' he demanded in a thin voice.

'Just look at that waistcoat,' said Belinda, prodding him rudely with one gloved finger. The waistcoat was new, of blue silk embroidered with garish yellow humming birds.

'What's up with it?'

'It's vulgar,' said Belinda. 'Too gaudy by half.'

'I am the very pink of fashion. Why, Lord Alvanay said he had never seen anything like it.'

'And neither has anyone else, sir. The yellow of the birds casts a light on your face which makes you look jaundiced.'

Saint Clair should have been glad of this new Belinda. But he felt like crying and longed to put his head down on the soft bosom of Mrs. Ingram and weep.

'I did not know you were a shrew,' he said acidly.

'I am not a shrew, but an intelligent woman whose eyes are offended by your dress.'

'Were we married, I would beat you!'

'Pooh,' said Belinda.

His face flamed and he turned the carriage around. 'I am taking you straight home, madam, and I expect a written apology from you.'

'Oh, really?' drawled Belinda. 'Then you may wait forever.'

Saint Clair had always considered himself an easygoing fellow, but he was angry as he had never been before. How dare this *bitch* insult his clothes. A red rage engulfed him, and he suddenly swung in his seat and slapped her across the face. Startled faces stared at them from all sides. Belinda burst into tears.

Shocked and alarmed, St. Clair said, 'I am truly sorry, but the provocation was great. You are never to speak to me like that again or it will be the worse for you.'

Belinda wept quietly beside him on the road home. Saint Clair began to feel quite manly. He had put this pert miss in her place.

*   *   *

Perry had cudgelled his brains to think of a way of getting rid of his cousin. The only reason St. Clair was getting married was because he was afraid of being disinherited. Perry had been following him for days and knew all about his clandestine visits to Mrs. Ingram.

If Toby, so his busy brain ran, thought he had an inheritance that would free him from dependence on his father, he would promptly try to end the engagement.

Then let him think he had money coming to him. That would get him out of Town, where he might be attacked. Perry drew out a plan of the

171

family tree. Saint Clair had no interest in family matters and probably did not know that Great-Aunt Amy had died the week before.

Perry travelled out of London to Hammersmith, where the great-aunt had lived. He found the large house had only a caretaker and wife in residence. He had taken the precaution of disguising his appearance. He introduced himself as Great-Aunt Amy's lawyer and said he had come to take inventory of the contents along with the heir. He would call in a week's time and would pay them an extra day's wages to leave him the keys and take themselves off.

This being successfully accomplished, he returned home. He then forged a letter supposed to come from Great-Aunt Amy's lawyer, telling Lord St. Clair that she had left her fortune to him. If he would call at her old home in a week's time at two in the afternoon, bringing his betrothed with him, they would both hear something to their advantage, Great-Aunt Amy having changed her will in his favour as soon as she had learned of his betrothal. He then sanded it and sealed it and sent it to St. Clair's town house.

The scene in the Park where St. Clair had struck his betrothed had made the gossip columns. Saint Clair sustained a visit from Lord Burfield, Belinda's brother-in-law, who threatened to horsewhip him if he ever laid a hand on Belinda again. Then St. Clair's father had raged at him for ungentlemanly behaviour and said he wanted the wedding brought forward to the autumn.

Lord Burfield's visit had convinced the terrified Lord St. Clair that there was no way out of this dreadful betrothal. He was convinced the Beverleys and their in-laws would sue him for breach of promise if he even hinted that he did not want to marry Belinda.

And then the lawyer's letter arrived. He immediately took it around to Mrs. Ingram. 'Do you see what this means?' he cried, his eyes shining. 'If I am financially independent; you and I can get married.'

Mrs. Ingram studied the letter. 'You are to take Belinda with you. That might mean that she is included in the bequest.'

'When in this day and age is money left to a woman?' said St. Clair.

Mrs. Ingram suddenly smiled at him. 'It was left to me and I have enough for both of us, but you will never countenance the idea of living on my money. But if you get your inheritance, it looks as if we shall have to go to Gretna.'

'A Scotch marriage. Just the thing. And Pa can do what he likes with that poxy Mannerling!'

*   *   *

Miss Trumble carefully cut out all the reports in the newspapers of St. Clair's scene with

173

Belinda in Hyde Park with her pair of sewing scissors. Then she pasted the cuttings on two sheets of paper, folded them, sealed them, and addressed them to the Marquess of Gyre at his country residence.

She quickly tucked the missive under the blotter as Belinda came into the room.

'You have not said a word to me in days,' said Belinda sadly. 'I would have thought Saint Clair's behaviour to me would have prompted you into speech.'

'I am determined to let you make your own decisions, Belinda,' said Miss Trumble, 'but now that you have brought the subject up, what prompted a lazy fop like Toby Saint Clair into such disgraceful behaviour?'

'The fact is,' said Belinda ruefully, 'that I was most dreadfully rude to him. I insulted his driving and his clothes.'

'Belinda!'

'I wanted him to take me in dislike.'

'Ah.'

'I should never have accepted him, Miss Trumble, and now what am I to do? The marriage is to be arranged for this autumn, and Saint Clair shows all signs of going through with it.'

'Then all I can suggest is that you summon up your courage and tell him that you do not wish to marry him.'

'There is some hope that it can be pleasantly done,' said Belinda. 'Saint Clair has just called

174

and he is very happy and excited. It seems that he had a great-aunt called Amy Wainfield, who lived in Hammersmith. She has left him her estate, which he thinks might be considerable. We are to go to Hammersmith to meet her lawyer for the reading of the will. Saint Clair said something like, 'Now I will be free and can run my own life.' You see, he is marrying me to please his father. If he has a great deal of money of his own, then he will not need his father's approval. So I decided to wait until the reading of the will and then tell him that I cannot marry him.'

'And what if all the old lady has left him is her lap-dog?'

'Then I must find the courage anyway. Shall we proceed to the grave as two old maids, Miss Trumble?'

'Better that than being trapped in an unhappy marriage.'

When Belinda had left, Miss Trumble put on her coat, retrieved the letter to Lord Gyre, and made her way over to the City to the main post office and sent it express. She did not entertain much hope. Gyre had probably already read about the scandal and had thought that Belinda Beverley was getting no more than she deserved.

* * *

A day later, Lord Gyre read the press cuttings

with amazement and horror. Some exaggerated and said St. Clair had punched his fiancé on the nose.

All the bad memories of Belinda that he had carefully nursed left his mind. The thought that St. Clair had actually laid hands on her was past bearing. Saint Clair should not be allowed to get away with it.

Lord Gyre went to the gun-room and lifted a box of duelling pistols from a glass case, tucked the box under his arm and went off to call to his servants to pack his bags and make his travelling-carriage ready.

*　　*　　*

Unaware of the wrath that was about to descend on him, St. Clair was showing the lawyer's letter to his friend, Mirabel Dauncey. Mirabel scanned the letter.

'Seems odd to me,' he said at last. 'This lawyer—what's his name, Fitzwilliam?—don't say nothing about how much. The old girl could have left you little. Did you know her well?'

'Only saw her about once when I was in short coats.'

'Then why should she leave you anything?'

'I don't know,' said St. Clair, exasperated. He had expected his best friend to be as excited and happy about the news as he was himself. 'I think it must be because she heard of my engagement.'

'Still plan to get shackled?'

Saint Clair had no intention of telling Mirabel about his love for Mrs. Ingram. 'Yes.'

'Why? She insulted you monstrously.'

'Belinda has been all right since then. Got to take a strong line with these females.'

'You amaze me. So this aunt lived at Bexley House in Hammersmith?'

'That's the place.'

'You go tomorrow?'

'Yes,' said St. Clair, 'and I hope the weather is fine.'

'What's the weather got to do with it?'

'I'll be driving my curricle.'

'Then, dear boy, if it rains, use the closed carriage.'

'We ain't married yet. Not the thing.'

'She'll have her maid with her at least, and you'll have grooms or that cheeky tiger of yours.'

Saint Clair shook his head. 'That lawyer wrote again and said the old lady had funny ideas and requested that only I and Belinda be there at the reading of the will.'

Mirabel raised his eyebrows. 'So you leave them outside or in the hall.'

'Look, old man, I am not going to put a foot wrong here. If I get my own money, I can tell Pa that from now on I'll lead my own life.'

'With a parcel of Beverleys around your neck for the rest of your life?'

Saint Clair laid one finger alongside his

nose. 'Let's just see what I get before we discuss that.'

*   *   *

Lord St. Clair let himself into his town house late that afternoon, planning to have a few bumpers of brandy and then change for the evening.

The footman who held open his drawing-room door for him informed him in a hushed whisper that the Marquess of Gyre was waiting for him.

'What's he want?' asked St. Clair curiously. 'Thought he was in the country.'

The footman did not reply.

Saint Clair walked in, the smile of welcome dying on his lips as he saw the black wrath on the face of his visitor.

'To what do I owe the honour ...' he was beginning as he bowed low.

Looking at St. Clair's foppish features, the marquess was suddenly engulfed by a wave of hate. He brought his fist up and slammed St. Clair right on the nose.

Saint Clair sat down on the floor, blood streaming down his face, and began to cry with shock and pain.

'I was going to call you out,' said Gyre, looming over him, 'but you are not worth the effort. Hear this. If you ever lay a hand on Belinda Beverley again, I shall kill you.'

178

'She insulted m-my c-clothes,' wailed St. Clair.

'And quite right, too, you miserable popinjay. Faugh! You make me sick. I shall be watching you.'

The marquess crashed out. After some time, St. Clair dried his tears and gingerly felt his swollen nose, finding to his amazement it was not broken. Then he proceeded to get well and truly drunk.

*   *   *

The following morning, the marquess went for an energetic gallop in Rotten Row. He wondered whether to call on Belinda. Now that he was in London, he longed to see her again.

He found he was riding in the direction of the Burfield town house. The streets of Mayfair were quiet as society slept off the excesses of the night before. But just as he had nearly reached the Burfields' house, he saw to his surprise Toby St. Clair assisting Belinda Beverley into a racing curricle. She looked pale and sad, and there were shadows under her eyes. The marquess' heart began to hammer. He put her downcast looks down to the fact that St. Clair was probably still beating her. And where were they driving off to without any servants or outriders?

He decided to follow at a discreet distance.

*   *   *

179

'What ever happened to your face?' Belinda was asking. 'You have been in a fight, have you not?'

'These things happen,' said St. Clair.

'Is it sore?'

'Of course it's sore, you empty-headed widgeon.'

'Good,' said Belinda.

'Fine wife you'll make!'

'You stink of brandy. No doubt you picked a fight when you were in your cups.'

'Just look at the scenery and keep that impertinent mouth of yours well and truly shut.'

Saint Clair and Belinda had fallen into the way of sniping at each other like a couple who have been married for years.

After half a mile, Belinda said, 'Can I ask you something?'

'Ask away, provided it isn't another of your damned insults.'

'Have you high hopes of this inheritance?'

'Very.'

'So if you inherit a great deal of money, you will not need to please your father any more.'

'Right.'

'I should be happy for you, if that were the case.'

He turned and glanced at her.

'I think you mean that. Why?'

Belinda decided then and there that she could not wait any longer. Perhaps if St. Clair found out that he had only inherited very little, then she might not have the courage to tell him the wedding was off.

'It would suit me very well,' said Belinda. 'I do not want to marry you. We should not suit. All this arguing is silly. I am so sorry I insulted you. You see, I wanted to give you a disgust of me.'

'You didn't mean all those things you said about my driving and my clothes?'

'No, I lied. But I do not want to marry you.'

Saint Clair reined in his team, swung round, grabbed hold of Belinda and planted an enthusiastic kiss on her cheek. 'I don't want to marry you either,' he cried. 'Oh, you wonderful lady!' He suddenly stared at her. 'Did you hope *I* would cry off?'

'Yes.' They both began to giggle like schoolchildren.

'Better drive on,' said St. Clair. 'I can just smell those bags and bags of money.'

Behind them, Lord Gyre made a half-turn to ride back to London. He had been sorely mistaken. They looked like the very picture of a young couple in love.

But somehow raging jealousy made him change his mind. Where were they going? And without servants?

*   *   *

The caretaker who let St. Clair and Belinda

into Bexley House had had his instructions. He was to take the couple to the upstairs drawing-room, serve them wine and cakes, and leave for the rest of the day with his wife.

The house was large and dark. Most of the outside walls were festooned with ivy, and Belinda thought, as they followed the caretaker up the stairs, that it was like walking under water as the moving leaves of the green ivy outside kept the inside in a flickering green submarine gloom.

'Mr. Fitzwilliam will be with you shortly,' said the caretaker. He indicated the decanter of wine, glasses, and plate of sliced cake on a table, bowed, and left.

'Just look at this place,' said St. Clair. They both looked about them in awe.

Stuffed heads of deer, foxes, and badgers stared down at them from the walls. The furniture was heavy and Jacobean: high carved chairs and a massive table gleaming like black glass with two centuries of polish. A huge grandfather clock ticked and tocked sonorously from the corner. Above the fireplace was the portrait of a lady in the dress of the last century. She had an autocratic face, bulbous eyes, and a contemptuous stare.

'Your great-aunt,' whispered Belinda.

'Fright, ain't she? I remember her now. Used to terrify me to death.'

Belinda giggled. 'Perhaps she has only left you that portrait?'

'Then I shall burn it. Imagine having those eyes staring at you, day in and day out. Let's have some wine. What is keeping that lawyer fellow?'

Lord Gyre had tethered his horse some way down the road from the house and then walked forward. A man who looked like a caretaker had let them in. He had not taken St. Clair's horses and curricle to the stables but had merely tethered the team to a post at the entrance to the short drive. Gyre, who had begun to fear a romantic assignation, began to relax. But what on earth were they doing?

He heard the clop of a horse's hooves coming along the quiet road and drew even farther back. He felt ashamed of himself now for spying on what appeared to be a supremely happy couple.

A man in lawyer's garb, his face shielded by a broad-brimmed hat worn over a bag-wig, dismounted and went into the house. Gyre was about to turn away when, to his surprise, the lawyer came out again and, after a furtive look all around, went round to the back of the house.

His curiosity now rampant, Gyre slid out of his hiding-place and went quietly round to the back of the house as well.

*   *   *

Inside, Belinda and St. Clair heard footsteps mounting the staircase and pausing outside the

183

drawing-room door. Both rose to their feet. Then there was the click of a key in the lock and they could hear the footsteps rapidly retreating.

'Well, what the deuce!' exclaimed St. Clair, striding to the door and trying to open it. He swung round, his face the picture of amazement. 'We've been locked in!'

'There must be some mistake,' cried Belinda.

'There isn't!'

Belinda ran to one of the windows, but they were mullioned and made of old bottle-glass. 'I can't see a thing,' she said desperately.

Saint Clair's face turned white in the gloom. 'Perry,' he said.

'Mr. Vane? What has he to do with this?'

'Only that Mrs. Ingram said she thought he would try to kill me.'

'Did you meet this lawyer?'

'No, I only had a couple of letters from him. Wait! What's that smell?'

'Smoke,' said Belinda in a hollow voice. 'I smell smoke.'

'We've got to get out of here!' St. Clair picked up a chair and smashed it against one of the windows, but the chair only bent the lead holding the little glass panes.

'Help!' screamed St. Clair. 'We're going to be roasted alive!'

*   *   *

184

Lord Gyre moved very quietly around the side of the house and then peered round the corner into the back garden.

The lawyer, if he was a lawyer, was piling bales of hay against the back of the house. Then he took a can of oil and began to splash the oil on the hay.

The marquess was to wonder often afterwards why he did not move more quickly, but he could not quite believe his eyes until the man took out a tinder-box. The first bale of hay went up in a sheet of flame.

Gyre ran forward. The man turned, and this time, despite the disguise, Gyre recognized the Honourable Peregrine Vane.

He threw himself on him, forcing him back into the burning hay, while Perry fought like a madman. Then finally the marquess was able to land one enormous punch and Perry lay still, his wig and his coat in flames. The marquess began to pull the burning hay away from the building, scattering it about the garden, jumping on it, cursing, demented with fear. He saw Perry's clothes were on fire, but could not bring himself to help him, in case the house went up and burned St. Clair and Belinda.

*　　　*　　　*

Perry regained consciousness. He brushed dizzily at his blazing clothes and then let out a shriek as a last great wave of pain engulfed him.

And then he began to smile. Because it had all been a bad dream and he was back at Mannerling, in the drawing-room, standing by the fireplace. A footman came in carrying a basket of logs.

'Fetch me some claret,' said Perry.

But the footman walked right through him, placed the logs beside the fire and walked out again, quietly closing the door behind him.

*　　*　　*

The marquess, seeing that the fire was not going to take hold of the house, then ran indoors and up the staircase, where he could hear St. Clair's cries for help. The key was still in the door. He swung it open.

'It was you, you bastard!' shrieked St. Clair and burst into tears.

'No, it was your cousin. I fear he is dead.'

'Mr. Vane?' asked Belinda through white lips.

She swayed slightly. He moved to take her in his arms and then backed away, saying instead, 'You are both safe now. How did this come about?'

*　　*　　*

It took some time for St. Clair to recover from his fright. When they were seated and drinking wine, St. Clair at last told Lord Gyre how he had been tricked.

186

'Someone will need to break the news to Earl Durbridge,' said Gyre. 'This will need to be hushed up. He will not want such a scandal. You have both had a bad fright, but now you are both safe and can look forward to your marriage.'

To his surprise, St. Clair's eyes filled with tears again and he said to Belinda, 'Oh, dear, now I am going to have to marry you after all.'

'No, you don't,' said Belinda. 'I don't want you, you don't want me.' A mischievous smile lit up her still white face. 'I know you want to marry Mrs. Ingram.'

'But I can't marry her unless I have money of my own.'

'Mrs. Ingram is a very wealthy woman,' said Belinda. 'Surely she will have enough for both of you.'

'But the shame and the scandal. Living off a woman!'

'It is done the whole time in society, I believe,' said Belinda drily.

'But I saw you on the road to Hammersmith,' said Lord Gyre, exasperated. 'You looked the picture of a happy couple.'

Saint Clair dried his eyes. 'That's because Belinda told me she didn't want to marry me and that was why she was being so rude to me. What were you doing, following us?'

'I wondered why you were both driving out of London without servants. Besides, you have gained a reputation for beating your fiancée. I was worried about her.'

'Well, we're deuced lucky you came,' said St. Clair. 'You saved our lives. You sure Perry is dead?'

'I think so. I will attend to matters here, Saint Clair. I think you will find when your father hears the whole story, he will be so shocked he will give you what you want.'

'He will never countenance a marriage to Mrs. Ingram.'

'Then you must be firm and tell him you are determined to marry her anyway.'

'Your poor hands,' exclaimed Belinda to Lord Gyre. 'You have been badly burned.'

'I will survive. Please go quickly. We will put about the story that Mr. Vane died in an unfortunate accident. I will need to find the caretaker and pay him to keep quiet. Please do go. The house is quite isolated but someone may have seen the smoke.'

*   *   *

Saint Clair and Belinda made their way slowly back to London. 'What a fright!' said St. Clair.

'Yes,' said Belinda in a little voice.

'Funny thing, you know,' said St. Clair cheerfully, 'I would have thought Gyre would have popped the question the minute he knew you were free. I mean, he came round last night and punched my nose because he'd heard I hit you. Then he follows us like a man obsessed.'

'I think Lord Gyre is heartily sick of the Beverley family and their ambitions to regain Mannerling,' said Belinda in a low voice. 'He is under the impression that if he proposed to me, I would ask him to buy Mannerling for me.'

'Never could understand the lot of you and that house. Great barn of a place in the middle of nowhere.'

For once, Belinda did not feel like leaping to the defence of her precious home. Mannerling had brought nothing to her family but humiliation and danger. If Lord Gyre had not followed them, they would probably have both been burned to death. No one would have ever found out who it was who had tricked them and Perry Vane would have become the owner of Mannerling.

*   *   *

Belinda told a horrified audience consisting of Miss Trumble and Barry, Lizzie and Lady Beverley, and Abigail and her husband, Burfield, of her adventure.

'This is dreadful,' said Lady Beverley faintly. 'Mr. Vane must have been mad and we never knew it.'

'He was driven mad by his desire for Mannerling,' said Miss Trumble.

'Well, at least he will never get his hands on it now,' said Lady Beverley. 'And Saint Clair and my beloved daughter will be there and—'

'Mama,' said Belinda quietly, 'I have told Lord Saint Clair that I will never marry him.'

'What? What? Oh, you are overset, my poor child, and do not know what you are saying.'

'On the contrary, Mama, that is the case. I have told Lord Saint Clair I do not want to marry him and he doesn't want to marry me either.'

And Lady Beverley, who had listened with surprising calm to Belinda's adventures, suddenly fainted dead away.

* * *

Shortly after Belinda had dropped her bombshell, Lord St. Clair was telling his story to Mrs. Ingram. When she had heard him out, she said, 'We had forgot to be on our guard. But it is over now. I think perhaps we should go to Gretna after all. I have enough money.'

'You know that would not answer. Pa would disinherit me.'

'But you have never cared much for anything other than enjoying yourself.'

'I care now, and demme, I don't see why I can't have you and my inheritance. Put on your best bonnet; we are going to call on Pa.'

* * *

They found another amazed and horrified audience in Earl Durbridge. Mrs. Ingram had chosen to wear a gown of irreproachable
190

modesty and a plain bonnet. She did hope St. Clair would have enough wit to turn his father's shock to his advantage.

'So you see, Pa,' said St. Clair finally, 'it was a day of shocks, for Belinda Beverley told me she doesn't want to marry me after all and I don't want to marry her.'

'Fustian!'

'I am going to marry Mrs. Ingram here.'

'What?'

'And you ain't going to stop me either. You were always holding your precious Perry up to me as a fine example. Look what your fine example turned out to be while I am damned as a useless fop.'

Bewildered, the earl looked at Mrs. Ingram, who said quietly, 'I love your son and will make him a good wife. I am a wealthy woman and we would not be a burden on your estate.'

'My son would live off his wife?'

Mrs. Ingram smiled sweetly. 'Only if you drive him to it. Lord Gyre is hushing up matters beautifully. There will be no scandal unless Lord Saint Clair and myself decide to be open about it.'

'Are you blackmailing me?' demanded the earl wrathfully.

'I am only showing you what a suitable member of your family I could be,' said Mrs. Ingram. 'You were quite happy to blackmail your son into marriage by threatening to cut off his inheritance. You were even prepared to countenance the Beverleys' schemes to regain Mannerling.'

'I suppose you want the place yourself,' sneered the earl.

'I hate the place. I don't want it.'

'I don't want it either,' said St. Clair, taking her hand. 'You should give me your blessing, Pa, and apologize to me for having held Perry up as a good example.'

His normally weak face looked quite determined. 'And furthermore, the Durbridge lands are by right mine, so don't be getting any mad ideas of leaving them to the kitchen cat!'

The earl put his head in his hands. Saint Clair and Mrs. Ingram waited. Then the earl pulled the bell-rope beside his chair and said to the footman who answered its summons, 'Fetch champagne. I have something to celebrate.'

*   *   *

Saint Clair returned to his town house sometime later, happy and tipsy. He flicked through the morning's post, which he had not yet opened. There were various invitations and then a large letter, of stiff parchment and with an unfamiliar seal. He cracked it open. It was from a reputable firm of lawyers in Lincoln's Inn Fields. They were honoured to inform his lordship that his late great-aunt, Amy Wainfield, had left him her considerable fortune.

Saint Clair fell to the floor, holding the letter above his head, kicking up his heels and laughing hysterically.

CHAPTER SEVEN

When I died last, and, Dear, I die
As often as from thee I go,
Though it be but an hour ago,
The lovers' hours be full eternity.
—JOHN DONNE

Belinda felt weary and sad. A whole week had gone by since the death of Mr. Vane, and yet Lord Gyre had not called. She feared he had gone back to the country. She curst her folly in having been so open with him about her silly ambitions. That very evening there was to be a grand ball at the Duke and Duchess of Hadshire's in Grosvenor Square. It was to be a glittering end to the Season.

She longed to cry off, to say she was ill, but Lizzie was so racked with guilt that Belinda was sure her sister would be made even more miserable by her not going. It was hard to put a brave face on things, to chatter to Lizzie as she was dressed in a new gown of silver tissue just as if her heart was not breaking.

Memories of Lord Gyre flooded her mind. She decided that once they were safely back at

Brookfield House, she would never look at or go near Mannerling again.

Lord St. Clair had called to tell her of his inheritance and of how Mannerling was once more to be sold. He and Mrs. Ingram were to be married before Christmas, and Belinda promised to dance at his wedding.

Mr. Vane's 'tragic accident' rated only one small paragraph in the *Morning Post.*

Belinda's downcast looks were understood by Lord and Lady Burfield to be a result of the ordeal she had gone through, but Lizzie and Miss Trumble fretted and worried about her.

'So what do you think?' demanded Miss Trumble of Barry. 'Is Gyre lost? He is still in London, I believe, and would normally be expected to be at the ball, but I fear he will not, and we will return to the country and that will be the end of that.'

'We could call,' said Barry slowly.

'I cannot even believe we tried to do that before. He is quite grand and I think he would regard it as the height of impertinence.'

Barry scratched his sparse grey hairs. 'Reckon it was my impression that his lordship rated you highly. Very open and frank he was with you, too. We could call and sound him out, like.'

'And yet I cannot understand why he did not promptly propose to Belinda. The man was head over heels in love with her, else why did he return to Town and follow her to

194

Hammersmith?'

'We'll never know unless we ask,' said Barry.
'No,' agreed Miss Trumble, 'we won't, will
we?'

*   *   *

Lord Gyre would indeed have proposed
marriage to Belinda Beverley, the very day
after he had rescued her, had not his friend,
Gurney Burke, decided to intercede. As soon
as he heard the story, Gurney realized that
Belinda was going to secure his best friend as
husband.

'For a nearly dowerless heiress, she is lucky,'
said Gurney. 'And think of being allied to that
family. Such a mother-in-law. Mannerling is to
be sold and they will never leave you alone
until you buy it.'

This brought forcibly to Gyre's mind all the
burning ambition that had possessed Belinda.
He remembered how Lizzie and Lady Beverley
had behaved to him at the opera.

How could he be sure that Belinda wanted
him for himself alone?

Still, he would have set out to at least call on
her after another day's hard thought had not
Gurney told him that it was well-known the
Beverley family were waiting for a proposal
because Belinda Beverley had failed at the
Season and Gyre was their last hope.

Had the marquess any vanity about his

looks, he might not have believed this fiction, but he had become accustomed to being valued for his lands, wealth, and title. And so he continued to avoid the Beverleys or any place he might meet them, and yet he could not bring himself to leave Town.

When Miss Trumble's card was sent up to him, he almost told his butler to inform the lady that he was not at home, but he pulled himself together when he remembered that the eminently sensible Miss Trumble had disapproved of the Beverley plots.

'Send her up,' he said.

Miss Trumble entered wearing a dark-gold dress of taffeta, an elegant bonnet, and a Norfolk shawl draped around her shoulders, carefully arranged in just the right modish folds.

She curtsied low to him, refused refreshment, and sat primly on a chair, her head a little on one side, her bright eyes studying him, he thought, with all the curiosity of a blackbird.

'To what do I owe the honour of this visit, Miss Trumble?'

'I am come to thank you for saving the life of Belinda Beverley.'

'That is kind and thoughtful of you, but Lord and Lady Burfield sent me a most charming letter to that effect.'

'And so Saint Clair is to marry his Mrs. Ingram. Highly sensible. It will be the making of that young man.'

'I think the most amusing thing that came out of the whole sorry affair,' said the marquess, 'was that Saint Clair did in fact get a substantial inheritance from his relative.'

Then followed a long silence while Lord Gyre studied the governess curiously. 'Why did you really call, Miss Trumble? It is ... er ... unusual for a lady to call on a gentleman at his home.'

Miss Trumble smiled. 'I am protected from scandal by age. Do you go to the ball tonight?'

'I am not sure whether I will or not. Why?'

'I just wondered ... Oh, this is ridiculous!' exclaimed Miss Trumble. 'Those wretched Beverley girls. Why should I care? But I do. Belinda Beverley is eating her heart out for you.'

'I find that hard to believe.'

'Why?'

'I was informed that the Beverleys expected me to propose marriage to her because I was their last hope.'

Miss Trumble frowned and looked down at her gloved hands. Then she gave a little sigh. 'They say all the world loves a lover, but I have never found that to be the case with a man's friends. The minute some gentleman contemplates marriage, his friends panic. So, do tell me, at which door was Mr. Burke listening when he overheard that?'

'How did you know it came from Gurney?'

197

'Who else would invent such a fiction? And it is a fiction. Use your common sense, my lord. When did Lady Beverley ever favour your suit? Lord and Lady Burfield are not schemers or plotters. They themselves married for love. When you hear bad news, always study the person who brings it to you. Mr. Burke once overheard an unfortunate conversation between Belinda and Lizzie and embellished it. Have you not always found Belinda painfully direct? Are you afraid she will ask you to buy Mannerling for her? This is Belinda Beverley we are discussing. Can you imagine her receiving a proposal of marriage and accepting that proposal only if you buy her Mannerling? I assure you, my lord, her declared intention is never to go near the place again. Oh, and in case Mr. Burke comes around with any more stories, I assure you he has not been near us, nor has he been at any function at which we were present. But if you tell him you are to go to that ball tonight, I am sure he will invent something else. Last night, we were all at home. We did not go anywhere, and today none of us venture out until the ball. I am telling you this so that if he says, 'Oh, I was at the opera last night and I overheard . . .,' that sort of thing, you will know he is out to make trouble.'

'Gurney has been my closest friend for many years. He did not try to interfere in my liaison with Mrs. Ingram, for example.'

'That was an affair, not marriage. Come, my

lord, where are your wits? If Belinda Beverley wanted Mannerling so much, would she ever have let Saint Clair go free?'

He looked at her with veiled eyes. How could he explain, to this prim spinster, the burning passion he felt for Belinda which addled his wits, his fear that his feelings could never be matched?

But almost as if she had read his thoughts, she said quietly, 'If you do not go to that ball tonight, my lord, you will never know and you may find too late that you have lost something of value.'

'I will think about it,' he said, suddenly formal. 'Thank you for your call, Miss Trumble.' He rose to his feet to show the interview was at an end. She rose as well, feeling suddenly as if she had failed.

'I did my best, Barry,' she said as they jolted their way back in a smelly hack.

'You can't do more than that, miss,' said Barry.

*   *   *

Miss Trumble herself arranged Belinda's hair for the ball, putting aside the Prince of Wales feathers that Lady Beverley had suggested and pinning silver roses in Belinda's hair instead. 'Feathers are so difficult to manage,' said Miss Trumble. 'Your gown is very fine. You will break hearts tonight, Belinda.'

Only my own, thought Belinda sadly. I will watch the door of the ballroom, waiting for him to arrive, but he will not come and the Season will be over.

'I wish you were coming with us,' she said instead.

'Barry and I are going to enjoy a pleasant game of whist,' said Miss Trumble.

'If only I could stay with you! I am weary of balls and parties.'

'This is the last one. A fine evening for it, too. A full moon. The Hadshires have a pretty garden at the back of the house where guests may stroll about the trees. So romantic. Why, I remember in the old duke's day, there was an evening ... Well, never mind. You don't want to hear an old lady prattling on. Courage, Belinda. You must shine tonight. Society will expect you to look sad because you have lost Saint Clair.'

'But I told *him* I could not marry him.'

'The Beverley ambitions to claw back Mannerling are too well-known. It is believed he did not want you, and so you must give the lie to that by looking as beautiful and happy as possible.'

'There is something evil about that house.'

'Mannerling? Yes, I would like to see the place razed to the ground.'

'Well, my good Miss Trumble, I shall try my best to shine this evening. Do you ... do you ever hear of Lord Gyre?'

'Only that he is still in Town,' said Miss Trumble calmly.

'We should have thanked him for saving my life.'

'Did Abigail not tell you? She and Lord Burfield wrote him a charming letter of thanks.'

'No, they did not. Mama would not, for she blames him for my turning Saint Clair down.'

'He has been thanked, so do not worry about it.'

He will not come tonight, thought Belinda, and all hope is gone.

*   *   *

Gurney called at Lord Gyre's town house to find that gentleman in full evening dress and placing a sapphire stickpin carefully among the snowy folds of his cravat.

'What's this?' he demanded. 'Are you going to the ball?'

'Yes,' said the marquess casually, 'I thought I might drop in.'

'You should have told me,' said Gurney. 'I must go home and change.'

'Why bother? You were the one who persuaded me that all these events were curst dull and I would be better off in the country.'

'Still . . . I was at the opera last night . . .'

'Oh, yes?'

'Belinda Beverley was there with her

mother, looking rather plain. I heard her demanding petulantly as to whether you had gone to the country or not. You had a lucky escape there.'

So what Miss Trumble had said was true, thought the marquess, his heart flooding with gladness. How could he have been such a fool?

He looked at Gurney with affection.

'Why don't you run along, Gurney? I am sure you will find that a quiet evening at the club would suit you better.'

'But I shall accompany you!'

'I don't need a nursemaid. Go away.'

'Oh, all right.' Gurney made for the door.

'Oh, and Gurney.'

'Yes.'

'I had one duel in my life. Do you remember? With Captain Johnson?'

'Yes?'

'You will remember it was because he told me lies about Mrs. Ingram being unfaithful to me. I do not like people who lie to me. Nor do I want to put a bullet through your heart. Do I make myself plain?'

Gurney turned dark red.

'I don't know what you're talking about!'

'Oh, yes, you do, my friend. You understand very well.'

*   *   *

Mindful of Miss Trumble's instructions,

Belinda danced with grace and smiled and chatted to her partners, keeping her eyes away from the doorway, and so she did not see the marquess arrive, did not know he was there until he was suddenly before her, asking if he might take her up for the waltz.

She turned red and then white. Her gloved hand in his trembled and as he swung her into the steps of the waltz, she gazed firmly at his chest. He tried to converse with her, asking whether she had recovered from the attempt on her life, but she answered in monosyllables, always keeping her eyes firmly on his chest.

He looked over her head to the gardens, spread out in the moonlight beyond the French windows, and made a sudden decision. He piloted her in the direction of the windows and, taking her hand, led her out into the gardens.

'Where are we going?' asked Belinda.

'Oh, so you *can* put one sentence together! We are going to talk, Belinda.'

They walked along a path under the moon. Little Chinese lanterns were strung through the trees and behind them, from the ballroom, came the sweet strains of the waltz.

'We will sit here,' he said, indicating a rustic bench.

They sat down together. The leaves of a sycamore tree above their heads sent moving patterns of light and shadow across his face.

He took both her hands in his and studied her bent head. 'Why do your hands tremble in mine, Belinda?'

'I am nervous, being alone here with you.'

'But I never made you nervous before, my bold minx.'

'I am still overset because of the attempt on my life.' She raised her eyes to his. 'I thank you from the bottom of my heart for saving my life.'

'And from the bottom of my heart I curse myself for a wasted romantic opportunity. Like a knight of old in the story books, I should have taken you in my arms and said, "Be mine!"'

Her lips quivered. 'Do not mock me.'

'I do not mock you.' He gathered her into his arms, and she gave a weary little sigh and leaned her head against his chest. He put a firm hand under her chin and pushed her face up. His head blotted out the moving leaves above, the Chinese lanterns and the shining room. And then his lips met hers and they plunged into a dark and private world of passion, holding on to each other, spinning together round and round into deeper, darker passion, deaf and blind to the sounds of the ballroom.

At last he raised his head and said huskily, 'How soon can we be married?'

Belinda clutched the lapels of his coat and gazed up at him with drowned eyes. 'As soon as you like.'

He fell to kissing her again while the orchestra in the ballroom struck up a lively country dance. And then somehow that dance was over by the time his wandering hands had found the delights of her breasts and the music from the ballroom was replaced by the chattering of many voices and the clatter of dishes from the supper-room.

He drew back at last. 'I go too far and too fast,' he said reluctantly. 'I have not even asked your mother's permission. What do you think she will say?'

'She will no doubt ask you to buy Mannerling.'

He stiffened. 'And you must tell her,' Belinda went on dreamily, 'that I hate the place and never want to see it again. I fact, I do not know what you are about, wanting to marry into such a mad family.'

'Because I am mad myself—about you.'

'But why did you stay away from me for so long?' asked Belinda. 'I was so lost and miserable.'

He hesitated. If he told her about Gurney, then it would be the end of a long friendship, for he felt sure Belinda would never forgive Gurney.

'I had to wait and get my thoughts together. I have always been courted for my title and fortune. And, my sweeting, all our conversations were about regaining Mannerling.'

'We will never speak of that place again!'

'Now we must go in, or they will wonder what has happened to us. But first, kiss me again!'

Lizzie's green eyes scanned the ballroom looking for Belinda. Lady Beverley was sitting with two old friends, immersed in conversation. During supper, Lizzie became even more anxious, and by the end of supper was feeling quite frantic. She searched throughout the house and then asked the footmen stationed in the hall whether they had seen a black-haired young lady in a silver tissue gown taking her leave. A footman told her that no one had left. The Hadshires' ball, he said haughtily, was the social event of the year.

Disconsolately, Lizzie trailed back to the ballroom and then she wondered whether Belinda had gone into the gardens. She made her way through the French windows and along one of the paths until she came across her sister locked in the arms of Lord Gyre.

Lizzie slowly backed away and turned and ran lightly back into the ballroom. Everything was all right again, she thought with a sigh of relief. Mannerling had not won. Then, she thought more practically, now I am the last one left and Mama will just have to let me wear my hair up.

*   *   *

Miss Trumble sensed there was someone in her bedchamber and came awake with a start. 'Who's there?' she called, drawing back the bed-curtains.

'Belinda,' said a voice from the darkness.

'Light the candles,' commanded the governess. 'I want to see your face.'

There was the scraping of a tinder-box and then a soft light bathed the room. Belinda came to the side of the bed and looked down at her governess.

'Oh, thank God,' said Miss Trumble. 'Gyre has proposed!'

Belinda sat down on the bed. 'Indeed he has.'

'Oh, my child, I am so happy, I do not know what to do. Yes, I do. Fetch me my wrapper. Over there on the chair. I am going to fetch Barry Wort and he can go to the cellars and bring up a bottle of champagne.'

Soon Barry and Belinda and Miss Trumble were drinking champagne in Miss Trumble's room. Barry and Miss Trumble demanded to hear what had happened and Belinda gave them a brief account, editing out all the kisses and caresses.

'Does Lady Beverley know?' asked Miss Trumble.

'Mama will know tomorrow when Lord Gyre calls. I did not want to spoil her evening.' Belinda began to giggle. 'Only imagine being afraid to tell your own mother that you have landed the catch of the Season!'

*   *   *

'Lord Gyre is called, my lady,' said the maid, Betty, the next afternoon, 'and is desirous to speak to you.'

'Oh, he no doubt wants to be thanked for saving Belinda's life,' grumbled Lady Beverley. 'I should have written to him, but I cannot help feeling if he had not interfered, then Belinda would have married Saint Clair.'

'Mad,' said Betty to Barry later. 'If it hadn't been for the marquess, Miss Belinda would be dead.'

Lady Beverley took her time changing and dressing and then made her way rather sulkily to the drawing-room.

Lord Gyre rose to meet her and bowed low. Lady Beverley waved a languid hand to indicate that he might be seated.

'We are most grateful to you, my lord,' she said in a bored voice, 'for having so nobly saved the life of our daughter.'

The royal 'we,' thought the marquess, amused.

'You are too kind,' he said. 'I am, in fact, called to ask your permission to pay my addresses to your daughter.'

'Belinda!'

'Yes, my lady.'

Lady Beverley stared at him. 'If you must, you must,' she said ungraciously. 'Belinda has been a sad disappointment to me.'

'Your daughter has not been a disappointment to me,' he said crossly. 'May I see her?'

She rose to her feet. 'Ironic, is it not, that Lord Saint Clair, who could have been my daughter's, is now going to marry your ex-mistress?'

She drifted from the room. I will make damn sure that woman never comes near us once we are married, thought Lord Gyre furiously.

Belinda came in and stood looking at him doubtfully. 'Was it worse than you imagined?'

'Much worse.'

'What can I do?' she asked helplessly.

He smiled and held out his arms.

'Kiss me better,' he said.

*   *   *

The wedding of Mrs. Ingram and Lord St. Clair was quite overshadowed by the wedding of Belinda Beverley to Lord Gyre. Lady Beverley had pleaded that a quiet wedding was all that was necessary, but Belinda's married sisters and their husbands had insisted on funding a grand one, and so Belinda was married at St. George's, Hanover Square, and as she walked down the aisle with her new husband, she could not help contrasting her happy lot with that poor young creature she had seen married before she had ever met Lord Gyre.

Belinda in white Brussels lace radiated happiness, but she confided to the marquess that now she was married she intended never to wear white again.

Her sisters noticed that Belinda at the wedding breakfast seemed to exhibit none of the bride nerves and each wondered privately whether Belinda was still a virgin.

Lizzie was wearing her hair up and Miss Trumble, looking at her fondly, thought that Lizzie would in her turn outshine them all.

But something happened to darken Lizzie's happiness. Her mother took her aside and told her that Miss Trumble had been dismissed. 'For it is you and only you who must try to get Mannerling back,' she said. 'And you are old enough now to dispense with the services of a governess.'

'But Miss Trumble promised to stay with us until I was married,' wailed Lizzie.

'Miss Trumble is a mere servant,' said Lady Beverley, 'and will do as she is told. She will return with us to the country to settle matters and then she will take her leave.'

'But where will she go?'

'That is not our concern.'

'You are only piqued because her gown and hat are more fashionable than yours, Mama,' said Lizzie.

'That is fustian,' said Lady Beverley, furious because her daughter had correctly hit on the source of her anger. 'Only see what a bad influence that woman has become. You have no respect for your own mother.'

'What will you do?' Barry asked Miss

Trumble. The servants had been allowed to join the wedding breakfast for a glass of champagne.

'I will think of something,' said Miss Trumble. 'I shall wear all my oldest gowns when we get back to Brookfield House and Lady Beverley will forget she ever dismissed me. Belinda is leaving now. We must say goodbye.'

They followed the crowd outside the house. The Beverley sisters were clustered together—Isabella, Jessica, Rachel and Abigail, Lizzie and Belinda. Then Belinda's husband took her hand and helped her into the carriage.

Miss Trumble felt tears pricking at her eyes and blinked them away. Another happy ending. She had long ago accepted that other people's happy endings were to be her lot in life.

Belinda waved and smiled. Her sisters waved back. Then Belinda sank back in the carriage seat next to her husband and said in a choked voice, 'If only Lizzie can be as happy as I am.'

'With Miss Trumble to look after her, I am sure she will. Now, come here and show me just how happy you are.'

To Belinda, the journey to the posting-house where they were to spend the night passed in a dizzy haze of long amorous kisses. They had planned to dine as soon as they arrived, but once they were alone together in their bedchamber, they somehow found themselves on the bed and their clothes on the floor.

'I am not very ladylike, am I?' asked Belinda at one point.

The Marquess of Gyre gathered his wife's naked body close in his arms.

'Thank God for that,' he said.

* * *

So Lizzie found herself alone and back at Brookfield House. Her only comfort was that Miss Trumble was still there. But the normally strong Miss Trumble had succumbed to a bad cold and was confined to her bed.

Slowly all Lizzie's curiosity about Mannerling began to come back. It would not hurt, she began to think, as lonely day followed lonely day, to just have one more look.

She set out one morning wearing a warm cloak over a wool dress and half-boots, telling her mother only that she was going for a short walk.

She knew Mannerling had been up for sale, but had heard nothing about there being a new owner.

She let herself in by the small side-gate beside the great gates of Mannerling. There was smoke rising from the lodge chimneys, but no one came out to ask her her business.

She walked up the long drive, a small figure with her long hair streaming down her back. There had been no point in putting it up when there were no social events to attend.

The front door stood open. Heart beating hard, Lizzie walked inside. In that moment, she knew she had made a mistake. All her love and longing for the place came flooding back. As if walking in a dream, she walked slowly up the great staircase to the first landing. The chandelier crystals began to tinkle and she swung round, alarmed. But the door was open, she reminded herself, and a breeze must be moving the crystals.

She went into the Green Saloon. How grand it had been in the days when they'd had balls here. Lizzie began to pirouette dreamily to the music in her head.

'What are you doing here, child?' demanded a haughty voice.

Startled, she turned and looked at the doorway.

A tall man, dressed in hunting-coat and top-boots, stood looking at her. He was hatless. His hair was thick and brown and worn in an old-fashioned style, being long and tied back with a ribbon. He had odd silvery-grey eyes under hooded lids, a proud nose and a harsh cruel mouth. He was very tall.

Lizzie bobbed a curtsy. 'I once lived here,' she said.

'That is no excuse for trespass,' he said coldly.

'But no one lives here.'

'This is my property and I must ask you to remove yourself. I do not want to be too abrupt. If you go to the kitchens, the housekeeper will no doubt find you some refreshment.'

Lizzie's face flamed as red as her hair.

'I am a Beverley,' she said haughtily. 'And the Beverleys do not visit the kitchens.'

'I have heard of the Beverleys,' he said coldly. 'Can't leave the place alone. I am Severnshire.'

So this was the Duke of Severnshire. 'But you don't need this place,' said Lizzie.

'I own many properties and this is now one of them. It will make a good hunting-box.'

'A hunting-box!' gasped Lizzie, outraged. 'Such as Mannerling is not a hunting-box.'

'Well, it is now, you impertinent little girl. Do run along or I shall have to ask my servants to turn you out.'

Lizzie turned and ran away. What a monster! How dare he speak to a Beverley thus!

On her return home, she longed to burst into Miss Trumble's bedchamber and tell her about the new, horrible owner of Mannerling, but dared not, as Miss Trumble would be furious with her for even going near Mannerling.

*   *   *

The following days were easier for Lizzie, for Miss Trumble was restored to health and

214

suggested she continue her lessons.

One day, two weeks after she had visited Mannerling, Lizzie was walking in the garden.

She heard the sound of carriage wheels on the road and ran eagerly to the gate, hoping one of her sisters might have decided to come on an impromptu visit. A grand carriage with a crest stood outside. Two tall liveried footmen let down the steps and opened the carriage door.

The Duke of Severnshire stepped down.

He looked down his nose at Lizzie and Lizzie glared back and then turned on her heel and walked back into the house.

'Who is that?' demanded Lady Beverley. 'I thought I heard a carriage.'

'It is the Duke of Severnshire.'

'Oh, my stars. Here! The great duke himself. And I have not even time to change my gown!'

Lady Beverley went outside. Lizzie reluctantly followed, suddenly curious to see why the monster had called.

'Oh, your grace,' cried Lady Beverley, dropping a full court curtsy while the duke responded with a curt nod. 'We are indeed honoured.'

'I am come to see my aunt,' he said testily.

Both Lady Beverley and Lizzie stared at him in amazement and then said in unison, 'YOUR AUNT!'

Behind them, Miss Trumble's quiet voice
215

said, 'What's amiss? Who has called?' And then she saw the duke. 'Oh, it's you, Gervase,' she said.

'And just what are you doing here, Aunt Letitia?' demanded the duke.

We hope you have enjoyed this Large Print book. Other Chivers Press or G.K. Hall & Co. Large Print books are available at your library or directly from the publishers.

For more information about current and forthcoming titles, please call or write, without obligation, to:

Chivers Press Limited
Windsor Bridge Road
Bath BA2 3AX
England
Tel. (01225) 335336

OR

G.K. Hall & Co.
P.O. Box 159
Thorndike, Maine 04986
USA
Tel. (800) 223-2336

All our Large Print titles are designed for easy reading, and all our books are made to last.

We hope you have enjoyed this Large Print book. Other Chivers Press or G.K. Hall & Co. Large Print books are available at your library or directly from the publishers.

For more information about current and forthcoming titles, please call or write without obligation, to:

Chivers Press Limited
Windsor Bridge Road
Bath BA2 3AX
England
Tel. (01225) 335336

OR

G.K. Hall & Co.
P.O. Box 159
Thorndike, Maine 04986
USA
Tel. (800) 223-2336

All our Large Print titles are designed for easy reading, and all our books are made to last.